The
PREACHER
and the Princess

The
PREACHER
and the Princess

"Fast paced, Down-to-Earth reading, Can hardly put it down..." – F. Stewart, Retired Educator, Former Aerospace Systems Analyst

Laura A. Franklin

THE PREACHER AND THE PRINCESS

iUniverse books may be ordered through booksellers or by contacting:

iUniverse
1663 Liberty Drive
Bloomington, IN 47403
www.iuniverse.com
1-800-Authors (1-800-288-4677)

Because of the dynamic nature of the Internet, any web addresses or links contained in this book may have changed since publication and may no longer be valid. The views expressed in this work are solely those of the author and do not necessarily reflect the views of the publisher, and the publisher hereby disclaims any responsibility for them.

Any people depicted in stock imagery provided by Thinkstock are models, and such images are being used for illustrative purposes only. Certain stock imagery © Thinkstock.

ISBN: 978-1-4917-7444-1 (sc)
ISBN: 978-1-4917-7445-8 (e)

Library of Congress Control Number: 2015912814

Print information available on the last page.

iUniverse rev. date: 12/11/2015

Contents

ACKNOWLEDGEMENTS

*F*IRST, I WOULD *like to thank my Lord and Savior Jesus Christ for the gift of writing and storytelling. This journey has been a long one. It has been one with hills to climb, storms to weather, and many, many in-depth conversations along the way, but He has sustained me. Without His guidance this wouldn't have happened. Thank you, Lord for reminding me that I was ready for this. To my Mudia; thank you for allowing God to use your singing voice through mine and for telling me that anything worth having is worth working for. This is worth it! To Frances Stewart: "Thank you" for being my eyes and ears by co-editing for and with me. Your insight and wisdom is priceless. To all of my family, extended family, relatives and friends: Thank you for sharing your life issues that helped shape this book, and I hope you enjoy the story. To Mr. Bill Escue; you were the first set of eyes I trusted without ever seeing or meeting you. Thank you for "not" understanding the African American community and correcting my Ebonics where you saw fit. Once we finally meet you will understand. To my children Jonathan, Jedidiah, Deion, Derick, and Mara: You are all the most beautiful gifts God ever gave me. I hope this story makes you wonder and laugh. To my big sister Liz: Thanks, Buddy, for the support and encouragement. To my little sister Vanessa: Thank you for listening to my ranting about this book for so many years. To the 'baddest' man in show choir, Dave Willert: Thank you for the advice and for stepping in when no one else would, and for never seeing color. Since my high school days you've consistently told me that I can do this! How wonderful for me to know* *someone like you. And now to the man who will forever have my heart; never junk, but a rare jewel in my crown. May the Informal Elegance that you project be captured in the hearts of all those you encounter. God Bless you. Thank you for the push. Thank you for the love. Thank you for the money, lol. Thank you, Daddy.*

Chapter One

MY BIG DAY

"YOU'RE GOING TO be late to your college graduation Harmony Wilkes, if you don't get a move on," Mrs. Wilkes said.

"I'm coming, Ma!" As Harmony is running down the stairs she loses her right shoe.

"Slow down girl!"

"Ma, have you seen the diamond bracelet Grandma gave me? I left it down here last night before I washed dishes." Even though Harmony was graduating from college, she still lived at home and she still had to do chores.

"Harmony, your father is waiting in the car for you!"

"Found it! See you there Ma." Harmony ran out the door and her mother watching her and smiling said, "She is so much like I was."

As the family and the other guests wait for the graduation to begin, Mrs. Wilkes spots Jacob looking for them.

"Over here," she said, waving her hands. "Hi baby. Did you get a good parking spot?"

"Yes, Ma," Jacob said. While discussing the events of the day, Pomp and Circumstance begins.

"Where is your father?" Asked Mrs. Wilkes.

"If I know Dad, he's probably taking a million pictures of Harmony," replied Jacob. "There he is," as Jacob waved his hands for his father to see him.

1

"Are you okay, John?" Mrs. Wilkes asked.

Wiping away the tears in his eyes, he said, "Yes, Belle, I'm fine. It seems like yesterday we were just at her high school graduation. She's grown up so fast."

The Chancellor finally gets to the end of the alphabet and announces, "Harmony Michelle Wilkes." A big roar sounded throughout the auditorium. Mr. Wilkes is taking more pictures.

While searching the crowd for Harmony, her family sees Asia and Rick, Harmony's best friends. Well, Asia is anyway. Rick is known as the neighborhood snitch, but when you really needed a guy to talk to without strings attached Rick was the one to go to. Harmony and Asia kept him on a need-to-know basis.

"I'm so proud of her," Asia said. "Man, I'll be glad when it's my turn."

"When will you graduate?" asked Mr. Wilkes.

"I'm outta here next year."

"And you Rick?" Mr. Wilkes asked.

Mr. Wilkes knew that Rick wasn't planning on going to college. Rick said it bothered him to get out of bed that early for school. Rick changed the subject to something regarding Mr. Wilkes losing weight. Mr. Wilkes knew that was his cue to leave Rick alone.

"Ahhh, there's my girl!" said Mrs. Wilkes.

"Ma, don't make such a big deal out of this," responded Harmony.

"Girl what you talkin' about? This is a big deal. Both my kids gettin' their degrees in engineering? Hush yo' mouth!"

Jacob reminds his parents that there is a celebration waiting at the house and that they need to head out.

"I'll take Harmony," Asia said.

"I'm ridin' wit y'all," Rick said.

"Okay, everybody else can go with my parents or me," Jacob said.

There were people from their church and the neighborhood waiting for the graduate at the Wilkes' home.

"Surprise!" they yelled.

"Wow Ma', you guys went all out."

"As if you didn't expect them to," Jacob said sarcastically.

"The place is beautiful Ma and Dad," Harmony said as she looked around. Harmony was greeted with hugs and kisses from the guests that had come to congratulate her. Time passed quickly. It was now 7 o'clock in the evening and a lot of the guests had already gone home.

"Let's start cleaning up y'all," Mrs. Wilkes said.

When she looked around, there was no one to be found except her husband asleep in the family room and a messy kitchen. Mrs. Wilkes got up, put a blanket over her husband, and went into the kitchen to clean up. Afterwards, she went upstairs to get ready for bed. As she said her prayers, she thanked God for allowing her and her family to see this day. She also thanked God for keeping Harmony focused through it all. Harmony had a rough freshman year in college. She had a boyfriend named Tony her senior year in high school. His young life ended when Tony and his friends were coming home from a graduation party. They were hit by a drunk driver. Tony died instantly. The others in the car had major injuries, but they survived. Harmony had a hard time forgiving herself for letting him ride with them instead of with her and Asia. She had planned to talk to Asia about getting more serious in the relationship and wanted advice. Asia reminded Harmony of who her father is, that he would kill her if he found out, and the possibility of giving up her virginity to a boy who barely started showing her attention in their senior year was ridiculous.

"Asia, you're still a virgin. How would you know?"

"So what, I'm waiting for Mr. Right," Asia said.

"Well, I finally have mine and I'm ready."

"Harmony you can't! Remember we said we'd wait until we were married?"

Harmony paused, rolled her eyes, looked over at Asia and said, "ok." They did their secret handshake and both agreed they'd wait.

Harmony's father tried to convince her that God obviously had another plan, but she didn't want to hear his words. Harmony's heart was shattered when Tony died. Harmony had always been the smart girl; a typical nerd. Education meant everything to her, and she wanted to make her parents proud. Throughout high school she stayed focused on her studies and her future. But when a six foot, four inch, athletic, good looking guy like Tony began to show interest in her mind as well as her looks, she was charmed immediately without question. The attention he showed her left her speechless and intrigued. Harmony felt she had been invisible all this time. She continued to carry a 4.4 grade point average, and finished at the top of her class, but Tony was definitely a welcomed distraction from studying. After the funeral she found out that Tony was using her to keep his grades up so he could graduate on time. Though it hurt to hear that news, Harmony was even more disappointed in herself for being willing to allow Tony to unwrap her gift too early. Mrs. Wilkes finished her prayers and went to bed.

The next morning, Mrs. Wilkes woke up to the sound of laughter and a loud television coming from the living room.

"Good morning, Ma," Harmony said.

"Hey, what time did y'all get in last night?" asked Mrs. Wilkes.

"We don't even know," said Rick.

"That late, huh?"

"Hey Ma? Can we borrow your car to go to the movies? Mine is out of gas."

"Sounds personal to me. Ms. Engineer, you need to save your money for gas in your own car. Well, okay, sure, but make sure you don't park anywhere where it can get broken into."

"Yes, ma'am," they all said.

Mr. Wilkes walks into the room to see what all the noise was about when he groaned about his back hurting.

"Good morning, Daddy," Harmony said.

"Good morning, Princess. How'd you sleep?"

"Apparently not at all," said Mrs. Wilkes.

"What?" replied Mr. Wilkes.

"Yeah, they got in pretty late."

"Well, she deserves some play time. She's worked hard in school. But, Harmony Michelle Wilkes?"

"Yes, Daddy?"

"Remember, as long as you live in this house, my rules still stand."

"Yes sir," she said.

Harmony had a great deal of respect for her mother and father and didn't want to damage the relationship.

"John, you okay?" Mrs. Wilkes asked.

"Yeah, that couch was hard on my back last night. Why didn't you wake me up?" said Mr. Wilkes.

"You looked so sweet and peaceful I couldn't bring myself to wake you." Mrs. Wilkes leaned in to give Mr. Wilkes a kiss.

"Ew!" said Asia, Harmony, Jacob and Rick.

Chapter Two

YOUR JOB *OR* YOUR FAMILY

A COUPLE OF MONTHS passed and Harmony had begun her new job at United Aerospace Incorporated where she also did her internship the previous year. She really liked the company. The benefits included a 401k plan, medical and dental coverage, an increase in responsibilities, and the possibility of traveling throughout the year. There was room to move up the corporate ladder as well. She knew that this was a man's world, but she would definitely leave her mark in it.

Harmony had a cubicle six feet by six feet with gray, carpeted walls. This area had everything she needed to function temporarily. She was the second assistant to Mr. Langston, the CEO of the company. Mr. Langston appeared to stand 5'11", and weighed 180 pounds. He was bald and very handsome. His eyes were oval-shaped and dark. There was a mystery about him. He was divorced with one son. He *looked* like he was around 44 years old. He never told any of us his age and no of us ever asked, at least not to his face. He was a stern man and ran a very tight ship.

Harmony didn't mind the strict schedule because she was ready to take on whatever any challenge thrown her way. That was until she met his first assistant John. John was fine! He was medium brown skinned, with dark eyes that made you wonder what he was thinking. His stance was a commanding one. John appeared to be six feet, four inches tall and weighed 200 pounds. He was bald also with a handsomely chiseled chin. He was well dressed and liked, apparently, because when he entered the office all the ladies would say in a resounding whine "Good Morning, Mr. Sutton." He would reply, "Good Morning, ladies." They all just giggled and went back to work. Harmony just shook her head and thought, "trifling women." His skin was without blemish and even-colored. He had the hands of a piano player; long, sleek, and toned. And he walked like he had a purpose; very precise with every step. While she was lost in the thought of him not wearing a wedding ring Mr. Sutton walked up to her.

"Good Morning."

With an ink pen between her teeth, Harmony replied, "hood-horning."

"What?"

Removing the pen and wiping the drool from her chin, she replied, "Good morning. I'm sorry, Mr. Sutton."

"Uh, please call me John."

"Okay, John."

"Are you ready for today's adventure?"

"Adventure?" Harmony asked.

"Well yes, each day here at United Aerospace is an adventure."

Harmony looked perplexed. John smiled at her as if to affirm her. "Walk with me Ms. Wilkes."

Harmony began to follow him and John began with the morning report as well as expectations for the day. Harmony made sure to bring along a writing pad and clipboard to take notes. Before she knew it, it was lunch time. John excused her for lunch and informed her they may talk at the end of the day. During lunch, Harmony met with Asia.

"How is your new job?"

"Fine girl. The man I work for is *fine too!* However, he is very demanding. But I can handle it."

"Aren't you worried about working for someone so good looking?" Asia asked. "No. I'm just making an observation."

"Okay, now, we don't want anything messin' this up. You've worked too hard." "Yeah, I hear ya. So where is Rick?"

"Girl, he said he was gonna try to find a job or somethin'."

"What?"

"Yeah, he said he's tired of being broke. He needs to go to cosmetology school and get his license. The boy's got talent. He just doesn't want to get up early in the morning."

"Well, if he gets his license and find a place to work, he can set his own hours. Okay, I gotta get back to work now. I don't want to be getting back late on my first day."

"Okay, love you girl. Bye!"

By the end of her first day, Harmony was feeling accomplished. She was able to keep up with Mr. Sutton's demands. He came out of his office and gave her an "A" for the day.

"Good work, Ms. Wilkes. Thank you. Uh, I think you can go home now. There isn't much more to do today. Monday's are usually full of meetings and basic projections for everyone for the week. Go home and rest up for tomorrow."

"Why do you say it like that?" Harmony asked.

"Tuesdays are very busy so bring a lunch. You might not leave the office until it's time to go home. Good night, Ms. Wilkes."

"Good night, John."

During dinner Harmony was discussing her day with her family. Jacob told her that she needed to run while she could 'cause she ain't gonna make it in that office with all of them women around one good looking man.

"You can do it baby!" said Mrs. Wilkes.

"Thanks Ma'."

"Princess, you deserve that job as much as anyone else. Your brother's just jealous 'cause he works with a bunch of men and no pretty ladies."

"Thanks daddy. I'm going to bed now. I've got an early day tomorrow."

She gave kisses to everyone except Jacob then went upstairs to bed. Harmony began her bedtime prayer.

"Dear Lord, thank you for this day. Thank you for my new job. Lord, I know you didn't bring me this far in my education and career to leave me, so I am asking that you continue to guide me and keep me and please bless Tony's family tonight and help me not to look at John in any other way except as my boss. Amen!"

Tuesday morning came faster than she expected. Harmony's clothes were already laid out, and all she had to do was say her morning prayers, get a quick shower, do her make-up and hair and then head to work. Harmony didn't have to fight the morning traffic because she rode the train to work. The morning commute on the train was crowded. She took an earlier train because she doesn't like being late. Due to this she had to stand for the entire ride. As she entered the office, Harmony saw that many of her co-workers were not in yet. She set off to prepare for her day. A quick prayer was said. She sharpened her pencils, turned on her computer, and waited for Mr. Sutton.

"Oh shoot, she thought, gotta go to the bathroom."

While in the ladies room, Harmony could overhear two of her co-workers, Shondra and Callie, making plans for the weekend.

"Girl, you goin' with us this weekend aren't you?"

"Nah, Callie girl. I got my own plans."

"What, reading another good book? You *need* to come with me to "The Spot" and get yo' freak on."

"All you do is talk about getting' yo' freak on. When you gonna stop thinkin' like that? That's how Jaylynn and Christopher got here."

"Look, I take good care of my kids. They don't want for anything!"

"Except a daddy," Shondra said sarcastically.

"Forget you. I'll go by myself!"

"Okay, Callie, I'll go with you. But I ain't drinkin' this time."

Just as they finished their conversation, Harmony walks out of the stall.

"Good morning ladies," she said.

They just looked at her as if she didn't matter.

"Good Mornin'." They both answered.

Harmony washed her hands and went back to her desk.

Later that day, she thought, Mr. Sutton was right, this day was busy. At one point during the day, Harmony had to call a time-out to catch her breath. Good thing she brought her lunch because she only had enough time to eat at her desk. She ate a turkey sandwich on wheat bread, light mayo, baked chips and a bottle of water. But she burned that off within two hours because of all the work she had to do. It was now 3:30 in the afternoon with only an hour and a half until this day was done. She hadn't seen John all day. She wondered if he even came into work. That is until she heard lots of giggles coming from the other end of the room. She looked over her cubicle wall and saw him coming her way. Only today, he wasn't smiling like yesterday.

"Ms. Wilkes?"

"Yes?"

"I need to speak with you. Walk with me."

"Yes sir."

Harmony followed him into his office. She had an anxious feeling in her stomach and didn't know what to expect. He closed the door behind them and asked her to have a seat but she didn't sit down. His office was stale. The walls were lily white. His desk was cherry wood. There was a pen holder on his desk made of black marble and brass with his name engraved on it. There were at least four bookshelves filled with books on mechanics, business management, and psychology. There was a beautiful silver and blue globe to the right of his desk, and he has an awesome view of the city. But where was his computer she thought and started looking around.

"It's in my desk."

"What?"

"My computer is in my desk. A lot of people wonder where it is. They think I don't work because they can't see it."

"Oh. Sorry"

Harmony was now embarrassed.

"Have a seat Ms. Wilkes. Yesterday was your first day, how'd you like it?"

"It was fine."

She tilted her head to the right and finished with her work day.

"It was a bit more than I expected. My internship last year prepared me for most of the work load, but not for the workload on this end of things. I expected to see Mr. Langston. I met him a few times last year."

"Let me tell you this," John said. "Mr. Langston only comes down here for three reasons: If something's wrong; for exercise; or to fire someone. If he doesn't speak to you, be glad."

"Oh, okay. I will."

"Now Ms. Wilkes we are always in crunch time in this office. Companies want their products and they want them on time and in excellent condition. There will be mounds of work that will require your attention and then you will pass the paperwork on to me. Then it goes to Mr. Langston. I'm going to need you to be very thorough, as if you were working for NASA. You're not being paid an entry salary of $60,000 a year to make mistakes. You gave excellent references on your application. They raved about you during your internship and that's why you're here. I don't need you to second guess yourself. Be on time. Finish on time. Always be ready for a shift in business. Each week brings a different load of paperwork and demands. And we must meet all of them."

With her eyes bugged out like a deer caught in headlights and a frown on her forehead, she said, "Yes sir, Mr. Sutton."

"John!"

"Um, John." She said.

"That'll be all Ms. Wilkes." Harmony had to understand that her job as Jr. Executive Officer of Quality Assurance was going to be demanding of her. She was not going to allow that to slip through her fingers. As she entered her workspace, Callie and Shondra were laughing.

"Only day two and you're already in his office?"

Harmony went back to her desk and continued working. And she worked quickly.

"It's quittin' time!" said Callie.

Harmony looked up and saw that it was 4:55p.m. She was so involved in her work that she lost track of time. She straightened up her desk, put on her tennis shoes, and headed for the train. On the ride home, she started doubting herself and whether she'd be able to handle these types of days every day. She looked out the window and quoted a scripture, "I can do all things through Christ who strengthens me." Philippians 4:13.

Harmony was glad to see her car. She dreamt of arriving home and soaking in a hot tub. As she walked into the house, she smelled something wonderful. Mrs. Wilkes was cooking.

"Ma! I'm home."

"Hi baby, how was work?"

"Long Ma'. I had a talk with my boss today."

"On day two?"

"Yep. He was just making sure that I knew what would be asked of me on a daily basis. Maybe it's because the last three people who held that position got fired for being lazy. They wanted the paycheck without doing the work."

"Well, he doesn't know you baby."

"That's what I said Ma'. What's for dinner?"

"Fried chicken for you and Jacob; baked for your father and me; Macaroni and cheese, string beans and ice tea."

"No cornbread?"

"Girl, you know your father won't go for not having his cornbread."

"I'm going up to my room to relax awhile. Call me when it's done."

"Okay baby."

It was 10:00 pm when Harmony woke up and ran downstairs. She was a little puzzled as to what was going on, and to find her mother and father were in the family room watching the news.

"Ma' why didn't you call me for dinner?"

"I did, but you never came down. I figured you were tired. There's a plate in the oven for you. Just clean up your mess when you're done."

"Thanks Ma'."

"Princess, are you going to be alright with this new job?"

"Yes. Daddy. I just didn't expect such a large work load in my first two days. I'll be fine. I'm a Wilkes."

Mr. Wilkes chuckled and said, "That's my girl."

"I'll have to bring some of my work home this weekend to stay ahead of the game."

"What? Princess we have a family outing this weekend. Did you forget?"

"Oh, that's right; we're going to Lake Moran. Well, I can just bring my work with me."

"No you won't," said Mr. Wilkes. "This is family time!"

"But daddy, I gotta stay ahead on this job. I have to prove to my boss that I can do it."

"Harmony Michelle Wilkes!"

Oh Lord she thought. Here it comes.

"Family is more important than your work. You know this is a family tradition. We go every year."

"Daddy, can't I just skip the lake this year?"

"My house! My rules!"

"But I'm grown now."

"Okay, then tell that to your new landlord."

"What new landlord?"

"The one you'll have when you move out next month."

"Dang! I'll make sure I have my sunscreen."

"I thought so," said Mr. Wilkes.

"You know your father wasn't gonna let you miss this. He looks forward to this every year 'cause you kids are always so busy. Family means everything to him."

"I know Ma'."

Mr. and Mrs. Wilkes headed upstairs to go to bed.

"Good night baby, Mrs. Wilkes said."

"Good night Ma'."

"Good night Princess."

"Good night daddy."

Harmony mumbled something under her breath as he leaves.

"I love you too, Harmony" her father said.

Chapter Three

WHEN IN DOUBT, ALWAYS PICK "C"

IT HAD BEEN six months now since Harmony started her new job. She had settled in very well. Her routine was simple; get to work on time, finish all the work on time, and go home. She found out through ear-hustling that Shondra and Callie didn't like her because she was *their* boss. The last one they had was a man and he was very handsome. Both tried their best to get a date with him, but he wasn't interested, and he was married. He just didn't wear his ring.

Harmony's team consisted of two women and two men. The two men who work under her are Ron and Danny. Both were very intelligent and creative. They were also supportive team players and were usually on time and met all of their deadlines. Ron and Danny had to answer to Harmony for many things. Neither of them minded because she was easy to work for. Harmony was assigned the task of organizing the annual office Christmas party. She recruited all of her team members to assist with the planning.

"Make sure we get the invitations out no later than Thanksgiving weekend. We want to put it in the minds of the other employees early on."

"That's *my* boss," said Ron, admiringly, but in a professional way. Shondra rolled her eyes.

"So, Ron, you bringing anyone?" Shondra asked.

"I'm not sure yet. Why?"

"I dunno. Just asking."

"What about you Ms. Wilkes? Are you bringing anyone?"

"It's Harmony. And no, I'm going stag. I don't need a man to have a good time." "What?" Callie said. "You like girls or somethin'?"

"No, I just know that I don't need a man to validate me at a Christmas party or anywhere else."

"Whoo-hoo, you tell 'em boss lady," Ron said.

"Shut up Ron," said Callie.

"Let's get back to work you guys. Now you all have your lists. Shondra and Danny will handle the music and the liquor. Callie, you and Ron have the food and the guest list. I will handle the hosting and hiring security. Are we all good?"

"Yeah, except why do you get the easiest job?" Callie asked.

"Because I'm the boss" she said firmly.

And with that, Harmony left the room and Callie's mouth was left hanging open. Harmony went to her desk feeling confident.

"Yep, "Today will be a great adventure." She said to herself.

Harmony met with John to let him know how things were going with the Christmas party. He was pleased with what he heard.

"Are you bringing anyone," he asked?

"No. What about you?"

"I'm not sure. My mother usually tries to set me up this time of year with women that she thinks will be a good mate for me. She figures if a woman gives me an expensive gift, then she has money and she's a keeper. But if she gets me something like a keychain, then she's probably broke and not very good marriage material."

"Are you serious?"

"Yes!"

"What does your father say?"

"Not much. He just lets her run on and on until she gets on his nerves and then he says, 'Meredith, leave the man alone. He's grown.' See, my father is what you call "old money." He was born with it, and in turn so was I. But because I chose to go to school and earn a living, my mother isn't too happy about it. I have a new position coming up in my life so she'll be fine as long as I choose the woman she wants."

"What new position?"

"As the Youth Minister."

Harmony tilted her head to the right and her mouth hung open.

"What?!" She replied.

"Yeah. No one here knows. I just keep it quiet because if people know I'm a minister, they'll want me to have mercy on them. But in the business world, there is no mercy, so the reverend part stays off of my name in the office but not out of my heart. At church I'm known as Reverend John Sutton, Jr."

"Wow! I wouldn't have pegged you for a minister."

"Why not?"

"You're so, so..."

"So what?"

"So stern and commanding, and kind of boring."

"Well, that's because Mr. Langston breathes down my neck, so I have to breathe down yours. But, I'm really a nice guy once you get to know me."

Smiling she says, "Okay, I'll take your word for it."

"Well, I have to get back to work. We'll talk later. Thanks Harmony."

While walking away she thought to herself, "Hmm, he called me by my first name."

"You're welcome John."

The day seemed to go by quickly after Harmony spoke with John. Knowing that her boss was a Christian man made a big difference to her. Not only was he fine and single; he was a Christian also. But he was her boss, and that meant she had to get rid of those thoughts. After leaving work, Harmony called Asia and told her to call Rick and for them to meet up at her house. She called her mom ahead of time to let her know they were coming over and asked if she could fix a roast. Anytime Harmony needed to talk, for some reason, she always ate pot roast. Mrs. Wilkes said that would be fine.

"Be careful coming home," she said.

"Okay Ma'."

Once Rick and Asia arrived they washed their hands, said grace, sat down at the table and started talking and eating.

"Girl, why we eatin' pot roast? Asia asked.

"Something's on your mind isn't it?" asked Rick.

"Yeah, yeah. I was talking to my boss today and I found out that he's a Christian!"

"Really?" both Asia and Rick said.

"Yeah, and he's a minister." Rick fell out of his chair.

"Boy, get up!" Harmony said.

"Listen, we had a nice long talk about how some of his life is and about his mother and father. His mother is kind of a prude, but his father seems nice; passive. John said he comes from old money."

"What's that?" Rick asked.

"That means he doesn't have to work if he doesn't want to," Asia said.

"He asked me if I was bringing anyone to the Christmas party and I told him no"

"So, what does that mean?"

"It means she's not bringing anyone to the party," Rick said.

"Come here, Rick," Mrs. Wilkes said.

"Yes, ma'am?"

She popped him upside his head and told him to go sit in the living room with Mr. Wilkes.

"Thanks, Ma'."

"You're welcome baby."

"Asia, what am I going to wear?"

"We'll find something. When's the party?"

"December 15th," replied Harmony.

"Okay, that gives us plenty of time to find something. "Harmony?"

"Huh?"

"Since when are you fussing about what to wear? You're not the kind of girl that gets all crazy over stuff like that."

"I know. I know. Okay, whatever we find will be fine. Let's eat, I'm starving."

The next few weeks went by fast and the date of the office Christmas party was getting closer. Thanksgiving had been fairly quiet. There wasn't a lot of family this year. No one felt like traveling, so everyone stayed at their own homes. The Christmas season was well under way.

It was a beautiful time of year and Harmony's favorite time of the year because she was born in December. Everything was going as planned. Ron and Callie had done a great job with the music and were able to get a really good price for the alcohol. Danny and Shondra had enough food coming to feed an army. Security would be in full force, and Harmony would be a beautiful hostess.

While Harmony was getting dressed, she got a call from Asia.

"Hey, are you sure you don't want me to go with you?"

"Nah, I don't want them thinking I like women. Plus, I'll be fine. I've got the Lord on my side."

"Well, when John sees you in that dress, you're gonna need the Lord and the twelve to hold him back."

Laughing she says, "Whatever girl. Thanks for helping me with everything. I'll call you tomorrow and give you the details."

"Okay, love you."

"Love you too, bye."

Harmony planned to arrive early to the party site and asked that her team do the same. It was to begin at 7 p.m. and her team arrived at 6p.m.

"Everything looks amazing! Great work!"

"Ow!" Ron and Danny said, simultaneously. "You look beautiful boss lady."

"Thanks you."

Harmony stood five feet seven and weighed 130 pounds. Her skin tone is like dark caramel and she has oval-shaped brown eyes and long eyelashes. Her seemingly perfect cheek bones and luminous smile lit up any room she entered. Her hair was in an up do with a sliver and rhinestone clip in the back. She was wearing a dress designed by Adrian West. The dress cost her more than she wanted to spend. It was black, satin and had rhinestones around the collar. It was conservative in the front, but not so conservative in the back. It fit her personality well.

"Where are Shondra and Callie?"

"Over there freshening up for Mr. Sutton."

Rubbing her hands together Harmony said, "Okay, well we haven't got much time before the guests arrive. Are we ready?"

"Yes!" they all responded.

"Okay Ron, start the music. Callie, make sure that once they look, sound or smell drunk, they get black coffee. Nobody drinks and drives on my watch. Shondra, stay on the caterers and make sure that the table always looks full."

Harmony clapped her hands twice and everybody moved to their prospective places. A couple of hours went by and all the guests were having a great time. Harmony was feeling glamorous - that is, until she saw John walk in the room with a woman on his arm. She was Caucasian, stood about 5'8" and looked like she weighed 140 pounds. She had dirty, dishwater blonde hair in a swoop to the right, and probably blue eyes she thought. She was gorgeous! She wore an Eloise Bay original. Those dresses were expensive. It was a fitted black and lame gold formal gown. The slit went so high up her right thigh that you didn't need to guess what she had on underneath, if anything.

"So I guess John's mom got her wish for tonight," she thought.

As John and his date came her way, she made sure she greeted them with a smile.

"Good evening, Mr. Sutton and this is?"

"Good evening, Ms. Wilkes. This is Laura."

With her hand extended to Laura Harmony said, "Nice to meet you. If there's anything I can get you, please let me know. Enjoy the party."

"Thank you." John said.

Harmony walked away disappointed. But she had to continue being the gracious host and present a vain act in order to keep the people happy. John noticed the back of her dress right away. She could feel the burn in her back. That alone was worth the price she paid for the dress. An hour passed, and she spotted John sitting at the bar alone. She walked over to him and started a conversation.

"Where's Laura?"

"Who cares?"

"What? You're not having any fun?"

"She was my mom's idea. She has money and my mother thought that if I bring her, then none of the women in my office would bother me."

"Do you ever tell your mother what you'd like in a woman?"

"No, it would just hurt her feelings."

"But what happens if she goes too far? How long will you allow her to choose your women for you?"

He looked at Harmony with a surprised look on his face.

"I'm sorry. I was way out of line."

"No, you're right. I need to stand up to her one of these days. Nice dress."

"Thank you."

"Nice tux."

"Thank you." John said.

There was a little nervous tension in the air. Laura walked up to the both of them.

"Sorry I took so long. Did you miss me?"

"I'll leave you two alone. Harmony said. Enjoy the rest of your evening."

After Harmony walks away, John's thoughts are perplexed throughout the rest of the evening.

"Uh, Laura. Why don't I take you home now?"

"Why what's wrong?"

"I don't feel well."

They left the party. Harmony just watched with a "feeling sorry for him" look *and* for herself on her face. An hour later Harmony noticed that the party was winding down, but she continued to be a gracious hostess. It was just about time to call it a night when Mr. Langston walked in with John at his side.

"Good evening, Mr. Langston. How are you?"

"Fine Ms. Wilkes. Nice party."

"Thank you Sir. Did you have a chance to mingle with the other employees?"

"No. I don't need to. I've seen enough. Good work. See you at the office."

"Good night Mr. Langston." They both said.

"I thought you left," Harmony asked John.

"I did. I took Laura home. All she talked about was her money. I gave her a scripture about how the love of money is the root of all evil."

"Yeah, I Timothy 6:10."

"How'd you know that?"

"You're not the only Christian in that office."

"Really?"

"Yep. I don't go around preaching to the team, but I do come in with an attitude of prayer each day."

"So what church do you attend?" John asked.

"Cornerstone Baptist Church. It's near downtown. What about you?"

"Um, Solid Rock Baptist Church. It's not too far from where I live."

"We're both Baptist huh? Nice."

"How about you attend church with me some time?" he asked.

"Won't your mother suspect something?"

"Probably, but I'll tell her the truth. I'll just tell her we work together and that we're just colleagues in the fight together."

They both laughed. Harmony agreed and let him know that she would let him know a couple of weeks ahead of time when it was a good time for her.

"I need to make sure everything is taken care of here before I leave." Harmony said.

"I'll wait with you to make sure you get to your car safely." John replied.

"Okay, thank you."

On the way to the car, John and Harmony talked about how they both ended up working for the same company. John's father knew Mr. Langston for a long time and he helped him get the job.

"Well, unlike you Mr. Sutton, I had to work hard to get in here."

"I worked. I earned my degrees."

"Yeah, but you didn't have to pound the pavement for two years looking for an internship."

"So does that make me a bad person?"

"No. I didn't mean it the wrong way."

"It's okay. I didn't take it the wrong way."

"Well, here's my car. Thanks for making sure I was safe."

"No problem."

"Good night, John."

"Good night, Harmony."

On the way home, she thought of how stimulating their conversation was. Instead of me forcing myself on him and possibly looking stupid I chose to wait on Christ to either make it happen or not make it happen. I'm not saying it's happening, but whatever happens, it will be God's will. Harmony began to pray on the way home.

"Thank you, Lord, for ordering my mouth tonight. Thank you for choosing my outfit and for helping me choose you. And thanks for allowing Mr. Langston to see the work I was capable of doing with the party. Please let me get home safely. I love you with all my heart and soul. In Jesus' name, Amen!"

It was New Year's Eve. Harmony was invited to go with Shondra, Callie and Ron to a night club, but she turned them down. Shondra and Callie enjoyed partying. Harmony said she'd rather spend that time with family and friends. Asia and Rick came over because they knew Mrs. Wilkes was cooking New Year's Eve favorites. She made black-eyed peas, chitterlings, macaroni and cheese, baked pork chops and of course cornbread. The doorbell rang.

"I'll get it," Harmony said. "It's Uncle Lionel."

Lionel was Mrs. Wilkes younger brother. He was also Harmony and Jacob's Sunday school teacher when they were in high school. He was 59 years old and widower. His wife died of ovarian cancer two years prior. It was a hard time for the family. Lionel stopped coming around as much because the family life reminded him too much of what he didn't have with his deceased wife Eleanor. Though he was teaching in the church where the family attended, he kept his distance throughout the year. He loved his sister and her family so he made sure he came around at least three times a year. He was a C.M.N.Y.E., Christmas, Mother's Day, and New Year's Eve man.

"Hey Little Brother! What you know good?"

"Not much. How are things with you?"

"Good. We missed you at the graduation."

"I know. I'm sorry. Here you go Babygirl."

"Thanks Uncle Lionel."

He handed Harmony $200 in cash. He didn't put it in a card or anything. He wasn't the formal type.

"Where's my brother-in-law?" Lionel asked.

"He went to the market for me," Mrs. Wilkes said.

"What about Jacob?"

"Out with some girl he's been seeing for about a month."

"Uh-oh," Lionel said. "You know what that means. Momma's and their boys. Nobody will ever be good enough for your Jacob, Belle."

"It's not like that. This young lady appears to come from a good family, but she's very controlling and demanding of him. I could see if they'd been together for a year or something. She wants Jacob to tell me half-truths."

"How do you know that?"

"'Cause Jacob tells me everything."

"Well, that's gonna change soon. I guarantee it!"

"Ma, what time are we leaving for Watch Night Service?"

"Probably around 9:30. You know how your daddy wants to get a good parking spot, and how those "saints" will be trying to get in to save themselves from whatever got them hooked this past year will be rushing in to get unhooked. And he doesn't like traffic."

"Okay, I'll be ready. Uncle Leo, you comin' with us this year?"

"Um, I'm not sure. I might have plans."

"You seeing someone Lionel?" asked Mrs. Wilkes.

"No Belle. It's just that I might have plans."

"What? You plan on watching the big ball fall in Times Square again?"

"I gotta go. I got things to do. See ya Babygirl! Tell Jacob I said hello. And your father too."

He gave his sister a kiss and told her not to worry. And that he'll be fine. Mrs. Wilkes just looked at her brother suffering, still, as he walked out the door. She knew he missed Eleanor, but what could she do. Trying to set him up with someone didn't work before so she just left it alone. She just prayed that he would somehow find some peace with all of it.

"Let's go Harmony! We're going to be late. You know how your father is about time." I don't understand these young folk Mrs. Wilkes thought to herself and shook her head.

"I'm comin' Ma'." Mr. Wilkes was leaning on the horn outside. "Did you turn everything off Ma?"

"Girl, don't be trying to stall by asking me about stuff I can do in my sleep." "Okay, let's go."

Church was packed. Jacob, Asia, Rick and Harmony sat with the Wilkes'. When the sermon was over, they finally said Amen and everyone stood up to bring the New Year in with prayer. Everyone clapped their hands, hugged and greeted one another with a side kiss on the cheek, and then went on home. On the way home Harmony's cell phone rang. It was John.

"Happy New Year, Harmony."

"John?" she asked nervously.

"Yeah, who did you think it was?"

"Well, I wasn't thinking it was anyone in particular. I just didn't expect to hear from you. I thought you'd be with Lorna."

"It's Laura." They both laughed.

"Well, I was driving home from church and I thought of you."

"Thanks for thinking of me."

"What are you doing for the rest of the night?" he asked.

"We're going to my house for dinner. What about you?"

"I'm going home. My mom and dad are taking a drive somewhere. They do it every year. They go to the very spot where they first kissed on New Year's."

"How sweet."

"Yeah, I know."

"Hold on John. Ma' and Dad, can I invite my boss over for dinner."

"Your boss?!" they both said.

"Yes," she answered.

"Why is he giving you a promotion if he gets to eat?"

"No daddy. He's got nowhere to go. Oh, daddy? Did I tell you he's a minister?" "Well, give him the address and tell him to take the streets with lights so he doesn't get lost."

Everyone in the car just laughed.

"Hello John? Do you want to have dinner with us?"

"Uh, yes. That would be nice."

"Okay, our address is 13151 Ramona Drive. I'll give you directions."

"No need. I have a navigation system in my car."

"Oh, okay. Can I bring anything?"

"No, everything's probably closed anyway. Just be careful."

"I will," he said. "And if I forget to tell you, thanks for inviting me."

"You're welcome. See you soon."

The rest of the evening, well morning, had a comfortable and relaxed atmosphere. Mr. Wilkes placed a log in the fireplace to keep it warm downstairs. Everyone had eaten way too much, and the fellowship was great. They all talked and talked and before they knew it, it was 3 a.m. Asia and Rick went into the den and fell asleep on the couch. Jacob snuck off to be with his girlfriend of one month. Mr. and Mrs. Wilkes went to bed and left Harmony and John to do the dishes.

"Thanks for your help, John. Even though I live at home, I still have chores."

"I think that's cool," John says.

"You do?"

"Yeah, that way you don't forget where you came from when you move out."

"Do you have chores?"

"No, but our housekeeper does."

"Wow!" she said.

"Listen, I won't forget where I came from just because I have someone doing my work. I know my grandparents and parents sacrificed a lot to get what we have. I won't take that for granted."

They finished the dishes and John and Harmony each had a puzzled look on their faces. The silence was uncomfortable.

"Hey, you want a blanket," Harmony asked.

"Huh?" John said.

"I meant for you to stay warm," Harmony said. You're not driving home this late. They have checkpoints everywhere."

"But I didn't drink anything except cranberry juice."

"Doesn't matter. If my mom and dad found out I let you leave this late, I'd get my butt whipped."

"Oh I'd pay to see that," John said.

"I bet you would. Around here, we treat all of our guests like family. That is until they act up and show their color. Then they get treated like the pool boy."

"You have a pool?"

"Nope! Come on," Harmony motioned to the living room. "We can just sit and talk if you'd like."

"Okay," John said.

Harmony decided to ask the first question.

"What made you go into engineering and business?"

"Well, when I was 10 years old, my dad and I used to get old pieces of wood and screws and just put things together. Nothing had a purpose. It was just something to do with my hands. But the finished product was a masterpiece; in my eyes anyway. I liked building things and figuring out how they work together.

When I turned 12, my dad showed me how to put a financial portfolio together and told me that if I didn't start saving now, I'd be broke by the time I was 18. I reminded my father of my age, but that didn't matter to him. He said we have to be good stewards of God's money."

"Really?" Harmony asked.

"Yeah. He's a minister too. In fact, he's the Pastor at our church."

"Aw man, you're a PK?" Harmony asked.

"What?" John asked.

"A Preacher's kid," Harmony said.

"Yes. I guess so."

"Well you know what they say about preacher's kids?" They just laughed.

"What about you?" John asked. "Why the degree in Engineering?"

"My dad is one and my grandfather was one," Harmony replied. "I am the official second son of my parents. I was a big tomboy growing up. Anything dealing with building things, electronics or just plain old using my imagination, I enjoyed. It was never about the money, but I'm sure I'll enjoy that too. When did you get your calling to preach John?"

"I was 20 years old and in my second year of college. I've always felt a tugging at my heart for ministry. I just didn't know I would be a preacher. I used to have dreams about it. I would dream that I was standing in front of the congregation saying something, but I couldn't hear myself. There were times when I would try on my dad's suits to see what it would be like, and I'd try to walk in his shoes. Even some of the elders in the church would say, 'boy you gonna' be just like yo' daddy'. I didn't understand what they meant so I ignored them.

The ultimate dream was the one I had when I was in my quiet time with the Lord one morning, and I was looking out of my window in my dorm room. I was admiring the different colors of the leaves and how God is so awesome to make so many different things. Then I asked the question of the Lord, "What can I do for you?" And it came as clear as a bell. The Spirit said, "Be my mouthpiece." I sat up in my bed and asked him to say it again. And I heard it again. "Be my mouthpiece." "I just cried. I cried out of excitement and fear. But not the fear of being afraid, but it was like a reverent kind of fear. I couldn't stop the tears," John explained. "I called my dad and asked him about it to get clarity and possibly confirmation. I knew the Lord had spoken to me, but you know how it is. All my dad did was cry too. He said he already knew, but that I had to find out for myself. That way, I'd believe it. And I did. And I still do."

"How did your family react when you told them?"

"My mom was thrilled! My little sister, Nettie was just a baby at the time."

"That's awesome, John!" Harmony said loudly. "Thanks for sharing that with me."

"Is Jacob your only sibling?" John asked.

"Yeah, thank God!"

"Why do you say that?"

"I don't think I could take having another big brother. He can be too protective sometimes."

"Aren't they all?" John asked.

"I guess so."

Harmony and John talked until the sun came up. They were still enjoying each other's company when Mr. Wilkes came downstairs and interrupted the calmness of the room.

"Good morning, Princess." Clearing his throat, "Um, John?"

"Sir? Good morning."

"Did you enjoy the uh, family last night?"

"Yes sir. Thank you."

With eyebrows raised and a concerned look on his face, Mr. Wilkes says, "But not too much I hope," giving Harmony *that* look.

"Daddy!" Harmony said.

"It's okay. I'd better be going now. Thank you so much, Mr. Wilkes for opening up your home to me last night."

"You're welcome son," Mr. Wilkes replied. "Be careful driving home."

"I will," John said.

"See you at work Monday, John," said Harmony. He leaned in to give Harmony a peck on the cheek, but she pulled back. There was a confused look on John's face and Harmony's. She stuck her hand out for him to shake instead.

"We're colleagues remember."

"Yes. And friends now, I hope," John said.

"Yes," Harmony answers. "Friends."

"Take care Ms. Wilkes."

"Take care Mr. Sutton."

She closed the door behind him and let out a long sigh. When she turned around she saw that everyone in the house, Jacob included, were standing right behind her.

"Oh my gosh!" Asia said. "He was here the entire night?"

"Yep!"

"And I fell asleep?"

"Yep!"

"What did he say to get you to let him stay here?" Rick said.

"Nothing."

"I asked him to stay. You know how my mom and dad are about letting folks leave late at night."

"Yeah, you lucky I wasn't here," Jacob said.

"Where were you?" asked Mr. Wilkes.

Harmony left to go upstairs and stuck her tongue out at Jacob as she walked by. While Mr. Wilkes gave Jacob a lecture, Asia and Harmony went up to her room to talk. They made Rick stay downstairs and referee Jacob and Mr. Wilkes.

Asia asked all of the usual questions. How was it? What did y'all talk about? "All y'all did all night was talk?"

Harmony only gave her little bits and pieces of the conversation. She considered what she and John shared to be private. And she felt privileged to have been the one he told. "The bottom line is," Harmony said, "when he leaned in to give me a peck on the cheek, I chose to pull away."

"What?" Asia said. "Have you lost your mind? That man is fine!"

"Yeah, I know. But if this is going to happen, it has to happen with Christ in the middle. And with Christ in the middle of us, we can't do a thing. I chose C."

"You chose what?"

"C! I choose to wait on Christ."

"Aw girl."

"What would Jesus do, Asia?"

"I don't know what Jesus would have done, but I know what I would have done."

"That's exactly why '*you*' don't have a man. Now, I'm going to get some sleep. You gon' hang out?"

"Yeah, I'll take another nap too."

"Well, you know where the pillows and blankets are. Hey, set the clock to wake me up at 2:00p.m."

"Why?" Asia asked.

"My mom and I are going to Shoemies for some work shoes for her and me."

"Okay, but I'll probably be gone by the time you wake up."

"Okay. Nitey Nite," Harmony said.

"You mean, mornin' mornin'."

"Oh yeah. Whatever."

Chapter Four

NEW YEAR! NEW YOU!

I T WAS MONDAY morning and Harmony was the first one in the office. On the ride into work she thought long and hard about what she wanted to do differently this year. She didn't need to lose any weight. Her body was curvy, in all the right places. Her *natural* hair flowed down her back. Whatever she felt she may lack in looks, she made up for in her intelligence. She took good care of herself and ate all of the right foods. Sometimes she'd pig out on junk food, but not too often. She was simple and beautiful. Harmony thought of herself as an easy-to-please kind of girl. She didn't need much to make her happy.

She went into the employee lounge and started a pot of coffee. She opened all of the blinds to let the winter sunshine in. It was a beautiful day to begin a new year. Harmony sat at her desk thinking about all the things that transpired on New Year's Eve with her family and with John. It didn't seem right for her to daydream about her boss, but nonetheless, she did. Callie came in complaining to Ron, Danny and Shondra about not having a good New Year's Eve and it interrupted her thoughts.

"Good Morning Boss Lady. How was your New Year's?" They all shouted.

"Good morning everyone. My New Year's was enjoyable. I spent the night with my family and a few friends."

"Man, I wonder who John was ringing in the New Year with," Callie said. "Probably some white girl," said Ron. "Probably that white girl he had at the party. Man, she was fine!"

"Shut up, Ron," Callie said.

"Hey Shondra, what did you do?"

"Well, I was curled up with a man named Ben and he brought his cousin named Jerry. Then we invited the twins E & J and had a good time." They all laughed.

"So basically what you're saying is that you got drunk and ate a whole carton of ice cream?"

"Pretty much," Shondra said. "I didn't have a date."

"Alright team, we've got work to do." Harmony broke up the mob around her cubicle and told them it was time to get busy. Though it was Monday, it was a busy day because they didn't work a lot between Christmas and New Year's Eve. While working on her files Harmony's phone rang.

"This is Harmony Wilkes."

"Good morning, Princess."

"Daddy! How are you?"

"I'm fine. I didn't get a chance to say good-bye to you this morning before you left."

"I'm sorry, Daddy. I was in a hurry."

"I understand, Princess. Say, are you too busy to have lunch with your dad today?"

"I'm never too busy for that. Where and what time?"

"Meet me at Dee-Dee's Café around 1:30."

"Okay, Daddy. See you then."

"Bye, Princess."

Harmony hung up the phone without saying good-bye. She saw that John had not been in his office all morning. Maybe he's got meetings all day. Before she knew it, it was almost 1:00 and Harmony didn't want to be late for lunch with her father. He was just as much a stickler for time as she was. Her father greeted her with a kiss and a long hug.

"So what's up Pops?"

"We haven't had lunch together in a long time Princess and you're getting older now, so I figured I'd better catch you while I can."

Uh-oh, she thought. He wants to talk.

"What's on your mind Dad?"

"Harmony, are you serious about this John character?"

"What? No! We're just friends, Daddy. Why?"

"I just got worried about the other night when he spent the night."

"He didn't *spend* the night, Daddy. He stayed because I know how you and mom are about people driving home when it gets too late."

"Oh. Well I don't want no man, preacher or not, taking advantage of you."

"I'm a big girl Dad. I can take care of myself."

"I know, but I'm your father and I love you."

"I know Daddy. Thanks. I love you too."

She got up from her seat and gave him a big hug. Lunch with her father was what they both needed. Harmony and her father had a strong bond; one that most girls could only dream of. Mr. Wilkes would do anything for his Princess. They talked about hoping Mrs. Wilkes would retire soon from teaching.

"The kids are starting to get to her," Mr. Wilkes said.

"Well Daddy, you knew mom loved teaching when you met her and those kids mean the world to her even if they do stress her out sometimes."

"I know, Princess. But I miss her at home during the day. Since I've retired, I've gotten bored."

"Why don't you get a hobby? You used to like building things. Why don't you build something for Ma that she needs around the house."

"Your mother has all she needs."

"Yeah, you're right. Well, it'll come to you Dad. I have to get going. I don't want to be late getting back. Thanks for lunch. I love you."

"You're welcome, Princess. Love you too. See you at home."

Harmony called Asia when she got back to her office and told her what her father said during lunch.

"Aw, that's too bad," Asia said. "Hey, maybe your dad can talk to Rick sometimes, since he's so bored. That boy ain't doing nothin'."

They laughed.

"Hey Asia, I was thinking of cutting my hair."

"What?"

"Calm down. It'll still touch my shoulders, and I want it layered."

"But your hair is beautiful. Do you know how many women would love to have your hair and have it to be their very own?"

"Yes. Well no. But I want a new look for the New Year."

"You mean a new look for the new man, right?"

"No, cutting my hair has nothing to do with John. It's just something I want to do for me."

"Uh-huh, well I don't think your parents are going to like it. Especially your dad after what you told me he said at lunch."

"I'll talk to my mom first and get her opinion. Then if she likes it, I'll let her tell my dad."

"What about Jacob?"

"What *about* Jacob? He's so involved with Ms. 'Do As I Say' that he won't even notice. I gotta go girl. I have a lot of work to do. Talk to you later. Love you."

Harmony hung up with Asia and went online to one of those sites that show you how a person looks with different hairstyles. While she was preoccupied with that, John walked up and startled her.

"What are you doin'?"

"Uh, nothing. Good afternoon, Mr. Sutton."

"Good afternoon, Ms. Wilkes. What's on today's report?"

Following him into his office, she gave him the run-down of all the clients that had sent in requisitions, invoices, and proofs for work.

"The only thing that's left to do is to pass them on to you and after you put your John Hancock on them, you can pass them over to Mr. Langston."

"Okay, good. Thanks." He never lifted his head from the paperwork. She just walked out with a funny look on her face. What was that all about, she thought? He didn't even look up at me. Oh well she thought. Back to work.

At quitting time, Harmony was still wondering what was up with John and his lack of conversation with her today so she went to his office to talk to him. She knocked on his office door but didn't get an answer. She knocked again and she heard him talking on the phone. Whomever he was talking to was making him very angry. He said something at the top of his voice and slammed the phone down. She opened the door cautiously.

"John, are you okay?" He didn't answer.

"John? What's going on? Is it Mr. Langston? Is there something wrong with a client?"

"No," he said. "That was my mother. We were arguing about me not coming home New Year's Eve."

"What!?"

"Yeah. I told her that I was fine and that I was with a friend. Of course to her that meant a "girlfriend." She thought I was with Laura. But I burst that bubble and she had a fit. I tried to tell her that I'm a grown man and she needed to stay out of my personal life. She said that she would not allow me to bring no low-life hussy into our family who didn't have her own money, and she quoted scriptures to me about children obeying their parents. She reminded me that that is the first commandment with a promise. My mother wanted to know whom I was with and where she lived because she was going to check her out."

"Did you tell her?" Harmony asked.

"No. I yelled back at her, and I don't remember the rest of what I said. Then I hung up and that's when you walked in. I am so frustrated, Harmony, with my mother trying to run my life."

"Well, that's because you are a grown man now and you realize that your mother has had way too much power in your life. You're like her "heir" to the throne so to speak."

"How do I get her to back off?"

"I don't know. Pray about it and ask God to show you."

"Can you pray with me?"

"Yes, but do you really think I should since I'm sort of in this equation. Maybe you should do it on your own so that you won't be distracted by me being here. I'll pray on my own for you, tonight, before I go to bed."

"Okay. Be careful going home," he said.

"I will. Thanks. Good night, John."

He waved her away and she walked out and closed the door behind her.

A couple of weeks passed and Harmony hadn't talked to John about anything except business. She had also talked to her mom during that time about getting her hair cut. Mrs. Wilkes didn't like it at first because the Wilkes women were known for their long, beautiful hair, but she gave Harmony her blessing. Telling her father would be something else. Mrs. Wilkes said she would handle Mr. Wilkes.

Harmony got her hair cut the following Saturday morning. Asia and Rick were with her. It was beautiful, they thought. When Harmony looked in the mirror, she started crying.

"What's wrong?" Rick asked.

"My hair is gone," Harmony said.

"Isn't that what you wanted?" Asia questioned. Asia then mumbled to Rick. "I knew we shouldn't have let her do it."

"It'll grow back," they both said.

Harmony cried more. Asia called Mrs. Wilkes and asked her if there was any more pot roast left.

"Yes. Why?" Mrs. Wilkes asked.

"Harmony's having a bad hair day."

"It'll be ready when you get here," Mrs. Wilkes said.

"Come on. Let's go home," said Asia.

When they arrived at Harmony's house, Mrs. Wilkes took Harmony into the bathroom and had a long talk with her.

"Girl, change can surprise us all. Sometimes we're ready, sometimes we're not. You weren't ready."

"How did you know, Ma?"

"Because I'm your mother. But now, you have to live with the changes you've made. Now, you're a Wilkes. You walk out there with your head up and show your daddy what you've done. And no matter what he says or does, you show him that you're fine with it. If you cry, then he'll cry."

"Over my hair, Ma?"

"Over anything concerning you and growing up," Mrs. Wilkes said.

Harmony washed her face and fixed her make up to look presentable. She went into the den to talk to her father.

"Hey, Daddy."

"What's up?" Mr. Wilkes looked up at his daughter and stared. He couldn't think of anything to say. He stood up, and went upstairs to his room.

"Ma!" Harmony cried out. "He just left and went upstairs."

"Oh Lord," Mrs. Wilkes said. "I'll talk to him. Go eat your roast with Asia and Rick."

Harmony didn't feel like eating so she just went for a walk with her friends.

"I blew it, you guys. My dad's gonna have a heart attack."

"Your dad loves you girl. He just can't accept the fact that you're growing up," Asia said.

"I don't think he likes my new haircut."

"Well, he has to," said Rick. "You can't just put it back on. Well, I guess you could sew it in," he said.

Both Asia and Harmony cut their eyes at him. Then they laughed because he was right.

"Hey, let's go back to the house y'all. I gotta talk to him."

As they approached the front door, Asia and Rick told her that they would see her later.

"Aren't y'all comin'?"

"Nope, Asia stated. "We know how your father is. But we got yo' back though. Call us later."

Harmony walked into the house and her father was downstairs again.

"Daddy, can we talk?"

"Yes, Harmony. What is it?"

She'd always been his princess. Now he was being formal. She swallowed hard and tried to assure her father that she was still his little girl; only with shorter hair.

"You're all grown up now," Mr. Wilkes said. "I guess I'd better start calling you by your real name."

"But, I'm still your princess, Daddy. I'm just an older one."

"Nah, it's time to stop calling you that."

Though Harmony was an adult, she still adored the fact that her father called her "Princess". He had told her that someday she would grow up and be a young lady and that whomever she married would have to treat her like a queen. But until then she'd be *his* princess. But now that's changed.

Harmony left her father's presence in tears and went to her mom. Mrs. Wilkes didn't say anything. She just hugged Harmony and tried to calm her down. Harmony went to bed early that night. In her prayers she said, "Dear Lord, what have I done? I feel like I have broken my father's heart. But I'm an adult now, right? I know my Daddy loves me. And I love him. Just like my mom said, I wasn't ready for the change in my life. I tried to make it happen without prayer. Even though it is just a haircut, it is still significant to my relationship with my family. I didn't consider whom it would affect. But come on Lord. I'm 24! I don't have to ask for permission for something as small as that, do I? I want to offer up a prayer for John and his family. They are going through a difficult time right now. Please bless him and the decisions he's making. I pray that both of our families will be able to accept the changes we've made in our lives. Though neither have anything to do with the other, please let everything be okay. I love my parents and I don't want to hurt them.

I love you more though and I don't want to hurt you either. Please let my hair grow back fast. Oh, I guess I shouldn't say that. Let my hair growing back be in your will and let John's decisions about his life be in your will as well. And just bless his momma 'cause she's not going to be easy to convince. Oh, and his dad too, 'cause he's married to her. Please forgive me for hurting them. Amen!"

Chapter Five

MOMMA NO!

IT HAD BEEN a few months now since the drama with Harmony's haircut and John's mom had begun. Soon Mrs. Wilkes would be on her weeklong break from school and Harmony would get a three-day weekend from work. The family would all be together for the first time in a long time. Harmony buried herself in her work. She and her team were very productive. In fact, they were so productive that they all got a spring bonus. They were given their bonus checks at the Monday morning meeting. Of course everyone was excited, and Ron and Danny 'proudly' professed that it was because of them that the team was so successful.

"Great work everyone," Mr. Sutton said. "That's the kind of numbers Mr. Langston likes to see. Meeting adjourned!"

All of them were headed back to their desks when Mr. Sutton called Harmony back to his office.

"Yes sir?"

"Close the door please. Have a seat. First, I want to tell you thanks for your help a few months back. I have spoken to my mother. We have agreed to disagree. My father tries to make her see that what she's doing is not right, but she is set in her ways and won't budge."

"What are you going to do?" Harmony asked.

"The same thing I've been doing since I talked to you. Pray. That's all I can do. I can't make her see things my way. She has to want to. And right now, she doesn't want to."

"What do you want?" Harmony asked.

"I want to tell you that I like your new haircut. It's very becoming of you. And ask if you'd like to go to church with me on Easter Sunday?"

"Well, thank you for the compliment and let me think about the Easter thing." "What do you need to think about?"

"Well, you know Easter Sunday is usually crowded with folks that haven't been there in a while. That's a big crowd to bring me into."

"We're not dating so what's the big deal."

"The big deal is your mother. And bringing me on such a significant day in the Christian world would mean something big to your family and your congregation."

"I don't have to bow down to them and explain myself nor my personal life."

"Actually you do. You are about to become the youth minister and you will have a very significant role in the church. You have to think about those things. Bringing a woman to church as a minister says one of two things. Either you're helping her get over some habit or you're looking to marry her."

"So what's wrong with the latter?" John asked.

Harmony just laughed.

"I'll pray about it. If the Lord says yes, then I'll go. If not, I'll see you at work the Monday after Easter."

Harmony talked to Asia on the phone about what she and John had talked about. "At least he likes your haircut."

"Is that all you got from the conversation, Asia?"

"No. I heard the rest. It's just that you got so much flak from your dad that I thought you needed some good news."

"Yeah, you're right. What are you doing for the long weekend?" Asia asked.

"I'll probably hang with my family and do some spring cleaning. My room has gotten junky since I've been working."

"You need help?"

"Nah, it'll give me a chance to clear my mind also. Plus, my mom has a doctor's appointment and she wants me to go with her."

"Is it anything serious?"

"I don't think so," Harmony said.

"Oh, okay. I'll call you later Harmony."

"Okay. Bye."

Mrs. Wilkes' appointment was at 4 o'clock. They made sure they were on time. Mrs. Wilkes had gone for a mammogram a week earlier and was waiting for her results. The radiologist thought that he might have seen something in the films that were taken, but wanted to be sure. The doctor took Mrs. Wilkes into his office. He told Mrs. Wilkes that they had found calcium clusters in her milk ducts and that they needed to do a biopsy to be sure the clusters were not cancerous. The biopsy was scheduled for the next day. Mrs. Wilkes was instructed to go to the lab for blood work. The lab technician told her not to eat after 6 am since the procedure was to take place at 11 am. Mrs. Wilkes and Harmony left the doctor's office quietly, holding hands. Both of them were praying in silence. Harmony took the keys from her mother so that she didn't have to drive.

"I'm not dead, Harmony Michelle Wilkes," her mother said.

"I know Ma'. I'm just trying to let you rest up for tomorrow."

"Give me my keys please."

Harmony handed her mother the keys and got into the car. The drive home was full of meaningless conversation between the two of them. Mrs. Wilkes asked about Harmony's job and how things were with John. Harmony asked her mother about how things were going with the kids at school and when she was going to retire.

"My spring break is coming up this week, so I'll be able to rest a bit. I'll retire when the Lord tells me to."

"Yes ma'am," Harmony responded.

They made it to the house in record time. When they went inside, Mr. Wilkes and Jacob were in the kitchen cooking up something that smelled awful. Mr. Wilkes knew how to cook, but it had been a long time, and there was no hope for Jacob. They were trying to keep busy while waiting for Mrs. Wilkes and Harmony to get home.

"How'd it go?" Jacob asked.

"It was fine," Mrs. Wilkes said.

Jacob could see on Harmony's face that it wasn't fine.

"Belle, what's wrong?" Mr. Wilkes asked.

"The doctor says he saw something in my mammogram last week and he wants to do a biopsy tomorrow."

"Tomorrow?" they both asked.

"Yes. I have to be there by 8:00 tomorrow morning."

"We'll all go with you," said Mr. Wilkes.

"That's not necessary," Belle said.

"Well, we're going, Ma. We're a family and we're doing this together." Harmony said.

Mrs. Wilkes couldn't argue with that. After dinner, Jacob and Harmony did the dishes to let their mom and dad have some time alone.

"How are you, Belle?"

"I'm fine, Joe. Just stop asking me about it please."

Mr. and Mrs. Wilkes got ready for bed and Mr. Wilkes said, "Let's pray."

Jacob and Harmony sat outside their parent's bedroom door and listened to their prayers and prayed with them in silence and held hands. After the prayer ended, Jacob and Harmony vowed that they would help them through this and no matter what; they would sacrifice whatever was necessary.

"We don't know what the biopsy's gonna show Jacob."

"It doesn't matter," Jacob replied. "We have to be there for Ma and Dad."

"Okay. We'll be there. Let's go to bed now and leave them alone," Harmony said.

"Good night, Jacob."

"Good night Harmony."

The next morning the air was tense, and everyone was walking on egg shells. Jacob, Harmony, and Mr. Wilkes took plenty of magazines to read while they waited on Mrs. Wilkes. The biopsy lasted over an hour. Mrs. Wilkes was a little weak afterwards and they took her out in a wheelchair. The doctor said the results would be available in two days.

"I put a rush on them. We'll talk soon" the doctor said.

"Thank you Doctor." Mr. Wilkes said.

Mr. Wilkes made sure he took streets that didn't have a lot of bumps so that Mrs. Wilkes would be comfortable. The location where the biopsy was done was extremely sore. When they arrived home, Jacob and Harmony made sure their mother wanted for nothing. Harmony informed them all that she would cook dinner and Jacob would wash the dishes. Harmony checked in at the office first to let John know what was going on and he said that he would say a prayer, and for her to take all the time she needed. Jacob alerted his girlfriend that he wouldn't be able to spend time with her for a few days until they knew the results of his mother's test. She wasn't too happy about it, but Jacob didn't care. For the next couple of days Mr. Wilkes just piddled around the house trying to stay focused and not dwell on the fact that his wife might have breast cancer. Mrs. Wilkes began to get frustrated with everyone and their silence so she called a family meeting.

"Look! I can't take y'all walking around as if saying the word "cancer" will make me explode. Whatever happens, God will take care of me. Now, Harmony, call Asia and Rick and tell them to get over here. And, I want you to go back to work because I won't have the results for a couple of days so there ain't no sense in you hangin' around here moping."

"Yes ma'am."

"Jacob, where is that controlling girl you like?"

"She's at work right now Ma."

"Well, call her and tell her to come over after she gets off. And, Joe, I'm going to need you to get a hobby and real soon."

"Yes dear."

"Okay! Get to work."

Everyone started moving as told. The next morning Harmony went back to work.

"What are you doing here?" John asked.

"Ma wouldn't let me stay home. It was driving her crazy for us to be hanging around and trying to stay busy."

"Hey, come into my office. I want to tell you something." Harmony followed him into his office. John takes both her hands, looks her in the eyes and speaks to her.

"Harmony, your mother is strong. No matter what, she'll be fine."

"That's what she said last night."

She didn't let go of John's hands.

"I said a prayer for her and for your entire family," John said.

"Thanks," Harmony said.

She began to walk away, but paused in mid-step.

"Uh John?"

"Yes?"

"I'll go to church with you on Easter Sunday."

"I thought you were going to wait for an answer."

"I just got it."

"Alright. We'll discuss the time later. Thank you for accepting."

"You're welcome, and thank you for asking."

Harmony left his office feeling better. Tomorrow would be the day they found out the results of Mrs. Wilkes' biopsy. That night at dinner, the Wilkes family talked about old stories of how Jacob had allowed Harmony to get hurt when they were little. Harmony wanted to ride Jacob's bike, but it was too big for her. Jacob let her ride it anyway to teach her a lesson. Harmony fell and cut her chin open. She was bleeding so much that he got worried. Mr. Wilkes gave Jacob the whipping of his life. She still has the scar from it.

Then Jacob told the story about how Harmony had gotten the whipping of her life when she took Jacob's homework and flushed it down the toilet, stopping it up and causing a flood in the house. They all laughed.

"Alright, I'll get the dishes," Mrs. Wilkes said.

"I'll help you," said Mr. Wilkes.

Jacob and Harmony said their good night's and went upstairs. Jacob and Harmony said a prayer for their mom and dad. They prayed that whatever the outcome, that God would guide them through it all.

Sitting in the waiting room of the doctor's office was nerve wrecking. The television was blaring. A show was on about baby mama drama. Kids were playing on the floor with toys. The phones were ringing. Too many things were going on at the same time. The receptionist came in.

"Belle Wilkes?" She called out.

"Over here," they all responded.

They were led into what is called the comfort room to wait for the doctor. The room was not what they expected. There was a giant screen television inside of a Cherry Oak Armoire. There were silk plants in the room of different colors. There was also a couch and a chair with floral print that matched the Cherry Oak.

Mrs. Wilkes' oncologist, Dr. Lee, came in to talk to the family. They held hands and waited to hear what he had to say.

"Mrs. Wilkes, do you want the good news or the bad news first?"

"The bad." She answered.

"The bad news is, it is cancer."

They all just gasped.

"The good news is, it's what's called pre-cancer. It's not threatening, but we need to get it out right away."

"Pre-cancer? Mrs. Wilkes responded. That's like being pre-pregnant. Do I have it or not Dr. Lee?"

"Yes Mrs. Wilkes. You do."

"How soon can we get this going? I have things to do?" Mrs. Wilkes said.

"My calendar is clear for the remainder of the week. We'll do it day after tomorrow. My nurse will give you all of the information about surgery and a list of things you can't eat or medicines you can't take for the next few days. After we finish here, I want you to go downstairs to have new lab work done. Please read everything carefully. You have two options Mrs. Wilkes. Either you can have a mastectomy or you can have a lumpectomy. Whatever you decide is up to you. You will have to undergo 36 treatments of radiation two weeks following your surgery. Everything will be done here at this facility so that you don't have to travel very far. A few days after surgery, you will be contacted by the Radiology Department to schedule your radiation treatments."

Pausing for a bit and giving everyone time to think Dr. Lee continued with his instructions.

"She will go through a series of different tests; an MRI that will check her body for any cancer cells that we may not have detected, and she will have what we call a marker inserted into the cancerous breast so that the surgeons will know where to cut. It will be a long process Mrs. Wilkes, but you're a very healthy woman, and I believe you will recover with minimal stress. If you think of any questions later on, give me a call." He handed them his business card, told them to take care and that he would see them soon.

The day after Easter, Mr. Wilkes thought, "Lord, surely if you got up on the third day, you can get rid my wife's of cancer in the same time. Let your will be done."

Harmony called John and told him when her mother's surgery was and that she wanted to spend this Easter with her family. Mrs. Wilkes would not allow Harmony to give up her plans to stay home with her. She made Harmony call him back and let him know that she would be there. John was glad, but also a little saddened by Mrs. Wilkes' dilemma.

"Y'all just say a prayer for me," Mrs. Wilkes said.

"We will Ma," said Harmony.

This Easter Sunday seemed more beautiful than last years. The weather was perfectly befitting for such a day. It was 70 degrees and the sky was clear. Mr. and Mrs. Wilkes, Jacob and his girlfriend went to Sonrise service. Mrs. Wilkes always enjoyed seeing the sun come up on Easter Sunday morning. The service and message was both moving and encouraging. She felt a sense of peace of what was to come. Afterwards, some of the women in the congregation who knew what Mrs. Wilkes was going through came over to offer their help. She said she'd call them if she needed anything. Mrs. Wilkes was a proud woman and didn't like asking, but she knew they were sincere with their offers. However, things at John's church were a lot different.

John walked in with Harmony and introduced her to his family. Mrs. Sutton greeted her with a painted-on smile. John's little sister, Nettie, was excited to see her. Pastor Sutton, John's father, gave her a hug. That caught Harmony off guard but was welcomed. John had to sit in the pulpit with his grandfather and father during the service. Harmony sat with Mrs. Sutton and Nettie. Nettie kept asking a lot of questions that were clearly none of her business. After all, she's 12 years old, and it is expected. While Pastor Sutton was reading scripture, Mrs. Sutton tried to show Harmony how to find books in the Bible. Harmony let her know that she was well acquainted with the word of God and that she'd be fine. Mrs. Sutton took that as her being flip, and Nettie laughed. After service John came over to where Harmony was to ask if everything was okay.

"I'm fine," she said.

"Was my mother rude to you?"

"Of course, but I let her know in a respectful way that I could hold my own."

John gave Harmony a high-five and motioned her to his grandfather.

"Grandpa Rufus, Grandma Maddie, this is Harmony."

They shook hands and greeted one another with a smile.

"Uh, Meredith, she reminds me of you when you were her age." Grandpa Rufus said.

"Only Meredith was a snob." Grandma Sutton said.

John's mother didn't like that, but it was true.

"Where are you from honey?" Grandma Maddie asked.

"I live in Westbrook, near downtown. John and I work together."

"Oh." she said.

"Harmony doesn't come from the same town as we do Mother Sutton."

"And where would that be Meredith?" Mother Sutton asked.

"Well, you know, from money," she said in a snobbish way.

"Meredith, John Sr. comes from money. You come from the fields of Arkansas. Now put your nose down and leave this girl alone."

With a wink to Harmony, Grandma Maddie continued speaking.

"She might be your daughter-in-law one day. Nice to meet you dear," said Mother Sutton.

"You too," said Harmony.

"Come along, Meredith." Pastor Sutton said.

When Mrs. Sutton walked away she was furious. Harmony asked John if he would take her home so she could check on her mother.

"Yes. Let's go." John said.

On the drive to Harmony's house John asked her how she liked the service.

"It was wonderful! The choir sang one of my favorites; "He got up!" But the best part was when your mother was told off by your grandparents. How long have your parents been married?"

"Thirty-three years, this June."

"Wow! Your dad has had to put up with her attitude that long?"

"He's kind of passive at home, but in the church, it's another thing. He lets my mother know her place."

"What about your grandparents?"

"They've been married for 51 years."

"So, marriages really work in your family huh?"

"Yeah, I guess they do. What about your parents Harmony?"

"Ma and Dad were high school sweethearts so they've been together for 32 years, but married for 29 years."

"Seems like we've both got longevity on our sides in the marriage department, huh?" John said.

"I guess we do." She responded.

When they arrived at the house and walked in, Mrs. Wilkes had just finished setting the table for dinner and they were just about to bless the food.

"Hey everybody!" They both said.

"Hey y'all." Everyone responded.

The house was crowded. It was Jacob and his girlfriend, Uncle Lionel, Asia and Rick.

"Why aren't you two with your family?" Harmony asked Asia and Rick.

"My family went out to eat with some people from church and I wanted your mom's food." Asia said.

"And I'm here 'cause my mom don't cook." Rick said.

"Okay, well we'll wash our hands first then we can bless the food with y'all."

Mr. Wilkes got ready to bless the food when John interrupted and asked if he could say it. Everybody looked around amazed, but Mr. Wilkes said that it would be fine.

"Then, let us pray," John said. "Dear Lord, thank you for this day. Thank you for your son dying on the cross and rising on the third day. We know that we wouldn't be anywhere without him. Lord, bless the Wilkes family and their friends at this time. I ask a special blessing on Mrs. Wilkes' body and that you would heal her perfectly. While she goes through surgery and treatment, keep her spirits up and sadness down. We lift her up to you right now. Hold this family in your hands dear Lord and never let them go. They are very important to me. Now, bless the food that we're about to receive for the nourishment of our bodies. Sanctify it and purify it. Please remove any impurities and use it for the strengthening of our bodies that we may glorify you. In Jesus' name. Amen!"

They all said a resounding "Amen" and sat down to eat.

"Nice prayer son," Mr. Wilkes said.

"It wasn't me," John said, "It was the Lord using me."

"Princess?"

"Yes Daddy?" Harmony answered with delight in her eyes.

"Pass the peas please."

Harmony got up and took the peas to her father and gave him a big hug. She whispered in his ear.

"I love you daddy." He whispered back to her.

"I love you too, Princess."

In a loud voice Mr. Wilkes said, "Let's eat!"

Chapter Six

MAMA'S BABY. PAPA'S MAYBE

I T WAS THE second week of May and they hadn't seen Jacob as much as they used to. He had gotten so involved with his girlfriend, LaTonya, that it seemed as if Jacob didn't exist. Finally, they'd found out what her name was. Initially, he just called her "my girlfriend." The family accepted her once she came to Easter dinner with him. She seemed like a pleasant girl, but Harmony was skeptical of her.

LaTonya was controlling with Jacob. She often told him that "what he wouldn't do, someone else would." He felt insecure with that kind of threat, so he was at her every beck and call. Harmony tried to tell Jacob she'd seen LaTonya with another man some time ago, but his nose was wide open, and anyone who spoke against her Jacob didn't listen to.

About two weeks later Mrs. Wilkes had finished her last treatment of radiaton, and Jacob called a family meeting. The family thought for sure he was going to announce that they were getting married.

"Ma, Dad. LaTonya's pregnant."

Mr. Wilkes nearly passed out.

"I knew it!" Harmony shouted. "I knew she was going to trap you!"

"Son, do you know if the baby is yours?" Mrs. Wilkes asked.

"Of course it's mine Ma." Jacob said. "I'm her one and only."

"Ha!" Harmony exclaimed. "I told you I saw that girl with this guy two months ago after y'all had that huge fight. I asked her about him and she said that it was her brother. Well, if I did with you what she was doing with him, I'd definitely be going to hell."

"Harmony!" Mr. Wilkes said. "Let's hear him out."

"Dad, I want to do right by her."

"And, what does that mean son?" Mrs. Wilkes asked.

"It means I want to marry her."

"Have you lost your mind!?" Harmony asked.

"Harmony, go take a walk." Mrs. Wilkes said.

"Ughhhh!" Harmony said.

She left the room gritting her teeth. After Harmony left, Mr. and Mrs. Wilkes had a long talk with Jacob.

"Son, think hard. Is this baby yours? Is it possible that she could have been with someone else right after you had that fight? She did say that "what you wouldn't do, someone else would."

"I don't know dad," Jacob said. "I guess it could be someone else's. But I'm scared. I really love her."

"I know you do. You owe it to yourself and the child to find out the truth. Call her and talk to her. Let her know that you won't go any further until you know the truth. But pray first and ask God to give you the right words to say. You don't want any unnecessary grief behind this."

While Jacob was calling LaTonya, Harmony was calling Asia and giving her the 411.

"Girl, didn't you say from the beginning that that girl was gonna trap him?"

"I sure did," Harmony said. "I hope my dad is convincing him to get a DNA test."

"Me too," Asia said. "So what's up with you tonight?"

"Nothing. I'm just going to hang around here and see what happens with Jacob. Girl, our family is going through a lot right now. Keep us in prayer. When's graduation for you Asia?"

"May 28th and I can't wait! I finally did it!"

"It feels good doesn't it?" Harmony asked.

"Yeah. It seems like it took me forever."

"But at least you hung in there and finished. A lot of people don't do that."

"How's your mom feeling?"

"She's doing well as far as we can tell. You know Ma. She won't tell us if she's hurting or anything. During her treatments, she was really tired all the time. Some of the ladies from the church came over with food and helped clean up and do laundry. At first, she tried to argue with them. That wasn't anything but pride. She realized she couldn't do it all by herself. My dad made sure she had everything she needed while she was recovering. I'm telling you Asia, my mom doesn't need this stress right now, not after all the stuff she's been through already."

"Well, Harmony, you're always saying how God can get you through any situation. He'll do it this time too."

"Yeah, you're right. Okay, I'm going downstairs to see what's going on with my big-head brother. Talk to you later."

"Okay. Bye."

"So, what did y'all decide?" Harmony asked.

"I'm going to go talk to LaTonya to get the truth about what happened and let her know that I want a DNA test right away so I can have some peace." Jacob said.

"Okay. You want me to go with you?" asked Harmony.

"Nah, you'll just cause more drama." Jacob stated.

While shadow boxing, Harmony said, "Well, let me know if you need some back up."

"Yeah, right," Jacob said.

As Jacob left, Harmony and her dad had a long talk.

"Daddy, what do you do if you know someone needs your help, but because they don't like you, they won't listen?"

"Ask yourself, what would Jesus do?"

"First of all, Jesus wouldn't ask about what to do."

"Harmony, who are you talking about?" Mr. Wilkes asked.

"It's a girl on my team. Her name is Callie. I hear her and another female co-worker, Shondra, talking all the time about their drama in and out of the office. They both party a lot, but Callie parties more than Shondra. Callie is a single mother with two kids. She says she takes good care of them and I believe she does, financially, but you never hear her talk about their father and whether or not he's in their lives. She doesn't even brag on them about things they've accomplished in school. I'm not trying to get into her business, it's just that it's affecting her work and as her boss, I need to let her know, but I don't want to come off in the wrong way."

"Well Princess, you could just pull her into your office and talk to her like a boss and then make conversation about her children. But pray first." Mr. Wilkes said.

"I will daddy. Thanks."

After the Monday morning meeting Harmony decided to talk to Callie during her lunch hour when the office would be empty of most of the employees.

"What's up Boss Lady?" Callie said.

"Callie, we've been working together almost a year now and you do great work."

"Thank you." Callie replied.

"But lately I've noticed a slight decrease in your performance. What do you have to say about that?"

"Well, Ms. Wilkes, a lot has been going on in my life."

Callie started to cry.

"Don't tell anyone, but the father of my children doesn't want anything to do with me anymore."

"What do you mean?" Harmony asked.

"He says that I party too much and that I need to concentrate more on being a mother. Ms. Wilkes, I take real good care of my kids. They don't want for anything. I buy them everything they ask for and more. All he does is take them to the park and spend a few dollars on them once in a while. That's not being a father."

"Is he the father of both the kids?" Harmony asked.

"Yes, I think so, but Charles, that's my man's name, isn't being fair by asking me to get a DNA test on Christopher, my youngest."

"So, why haven't you gotten a paternity test done on Christopher?"

"Because I know who the father is and I'm not having him try to run my life."

"Why would he question the paternity then?"

"See, he and I had a fight awhile back. I thought he was seeing this white girl from across town. He said they were only friends and that they work together. But she didn't look like any of my friends so I went up to them and just asked him out loud. Charles told me that I was embarrassing him and asked me to leave. I wouldn't leave so security came and escorted me away, and Charles didn't come home for three days. Since he didn't come home, I called my friend; a friend from back in the day. It wasn't nothin', just a comfort thing. Well, too much kissing and too many drinks later and then, well you know. But then Charles finally came home, and we made love. He said that maybe we should break up because I was stressing him out. Can you believe this? All after what we did? And it was good too."

"Are you two married, Callie?"

"No, but I was hoping that one day he would ask me."

"Let me ask you something Callie. Do you go to church?"

"No. Why?"

"Do you believe in God?"

"Yeah. Why?"

"Are you saved?"

Callie was aggravated by the questions.

"Yeah. Why!?"

"Maybe what you need to do is to get your relationship right with God, and then your other relationships will come together."

"Look, I didn't come in here for a sermon, boss lady."

"And, I'm not going to give you one. But as your boss, I am obligated to tell you that you're not too far from collecting unemployment. And, as your Christian sister in the fight, I am obligated to tell you that if you don't get your life together with God soon, you could possibly lose more than you're willing to. See Callie, God only gives us so many chances to make things right. Then after a while, he will get tired of waiting. Don't allow your outward circumstances to change the inward reality. Get yourself and your family in a church where your children can grow spiritually and hang out and grow in Christ with kids their age. And, where you can get your praise on and trust God to do His thing.

Don't worry so much about what Charles is or isn't doing. Once he sees the change in you, he might come around. But if he doesn't, then that's fine too. But you have to be okay with it. The kids can't choose for themselves right now. It's up to you; not you and yo' man. Now, what's said in this office stays here. And I won't share anything with anyone, but the fact that I talked to you about your job performance will go into your file. I'll need you to sign this form stating that we did discuss your future here at United Aerospace Inc. Callie?"

"Yes?"

"Stop sharing all of your business with the people in this office. I know you and Shondra are close and that's fine, but share between you two, not between the twelve of us. Trust me when I say that everybody smiling in your face is not your friend. Okay, we're done here. You still have time to get you something to eat if you'd like."

"Thanks Ms. Wilkes."

"Behind these doors you can call me Harmony. But elsewhere, it's Ms. Wilkes. I don't want you gettin' beside yourself."

Callie wiped her tears, looked in the mirror on the wall and walked out laughing. After Callie left the office Harmony just said, "Thank you Jesus. I've planted the seed, now it's your turn."

Back at the house, Jacob and Mr. Wilkes were having lunch when the phone rang. It was Harmony.

"What happened big brother?"

"After a long talk with LaTonya, she finally agreed to take the test. We go tomorrow and the results will be ready in about a week. Harm?"

"Yeah?"

"Thanks for having my back. I know you were only looking out for me and I've told Ma and Dad that I'm sorry for causing all of this stress. Especially since Ma doesn't need it right now. And I'm sorry to you too."

"For what?" Harmony asked.

"For calling you names behind your back. Something in me told me that LaTonya was playing games with me, but I'm in love with her."

"Jacob, love isn't playing games with people's feelings or their hearts. And it sure isn't being controlling over your mate's life. If you really love her, then let her know that some things need to change. And if she loves you like she says she does, she will do it. Maybe this baby coming is a good thing, whether it's yours or not. God always has a plan. We just have to allow ourselves to be a part of it."

"I know sis. Thanks. You always did know what to say to me to make me feel better. I'll let what you said marinate awhile."

"Okay, tell Dad and Ma hi, and I'll be home right after work. Love you Big Bro."

"Love you too."

"So what did Harmony say?" Mr. Wilkes asked.

"Just gave me some sisterly advice. I hope John knows what kind of woman he's getting," Jacob said.

"What do you mean by that?" asked Mr. Wilkes.

Chapter Seven

THE GRACE OF GOD

"Ma?" "Yes Harmony?"

"Are you going to Asia's graduation?"

"I'm not sure yet. What time does it start?"

"Five o'clock tonight, but Rick and I are leaving here around four to get a good parking spot."

"It's only ten in the morning, so I've got some time to rest a while. I'm gonna lie down after I do this load of laundry."

"Okay Ma. You want me to help you?" Harmony asked.

"No, I'll be fine," Mrs. Wilkes said. "You go on."

"Okay, I'll check on you later."

After Harmony left her mother, she went upstairs to talk with her father.

"Dad, is Ma okay?"

"Yes. Why?"

"She always seems so tired."

"Well, remember that's from the radiation treatments. Although her treatments are over, it still takes a toll on her physically for at least three to four more months."

"Can we do anything for her?" Harmony asked.

"No. It just has to run its course. And you know your mother is too proud to ask for help."

"I know," Harmony said. "I'm getting ready to go with Rick to pick up Asia's graduation gift. Can I do anything for you before I leave or while I'm gone?"

"No Princess. We're fine."

"Okay, I'll only be gone for a couple of hours."

Harmony went over and gave her father a kiss before she left.

"Drive safely." Mr. Wilkes said.

"I will."

She went downstairs to give her mom a kiss as well and told her good-bye.

Rick and Harmony decided to give Asia a gift certificate of $200 for graduation. She had worked hard in school and they couldn't agree on what to get her. But Harmony got Asia another gift also, as her best friend. Harmony dropped Rick off at home and then went on to her house. Her cell phone rang. It was John.

"Hey you!" He said.

"Hey yourself!" She replied with excitement.

"What are you up to?"

"I'm headed home from dropping off Rick."

"What time is the graduation?" John asked.

"It begins at five."

"Oh, I see. Do you have time for a visitor before you get ready?" John asked.

"Sure. Can you give me time to get home and check on my family first? Ma looked a little tired when I left."

"Okay, how does an hour sound?"

"That's good for me."

"See you soon." John said.

Harmony rushed home to see if her parents needed anything before she got dressed for John's arrival. She alerted her parents that John was coming over and not to worry about him staying too long.

"He's just coming for a short visit," Harmony said.

Mr. and Mrs. Wilkes said that that would be fine.

Harmony decided to wear a light blue sun dress with tan, open toe sandals and a white bolero jacket. She didn't know what he was wearing, but she didn't want to look too eager to see him. The doorbell rang and Mr. Wilkes said that he would answer the door for her.

"Good evening Mr. Wilkes. How are you?"

"Good evening John. I'm fine and you?"

"Good sir."

"Please come in. Harmony's upstairs. I'll get her." Mr. Wilkes went to the bottom of the stairs and called out, "Harmony?"

"Yes Dad?"

"John's here to see you."

"I'll be right down."

Mr. Wilkes went into the den to give them some privacy. When Harmony started down the stairs, John stood up to meet her at the bottom. She was so caught up in trying to be cute that she lost her footing at the bottom of the stairs and began to fall. John was able to catch her.

"Are you alright?" John asked.

"Yeah, thanks for catching me. That would not have been pretty."

"If I'd known you'd fall for me this quickly," John said, "I would have asked you out earlier." They both laughed.

"Are you okay, Princess?" Mr. Wilkes asked, emerging from the den after hearing the commotion.

"Yeah Dad. I just lost my footing coming down the stairs."

Harmony, being grateful that John had spared her some embarrassment, graciously gave him a "pat-pat release" hug. This is also known as a "Holy Hug."

"Have a seat," she told him.

Mr. Wilkes retreated back to the den.

"What's going on?" Harmony asked.

"I was just in the neighborhood and thought of you." John said.

"Really? John, you live 45 minutes away."

"Okay," he said. "You caught me. I really wanted to see you and give you these."

He handed her three roses of different colors. He told her that the white one was for her heart. The yellow one was for their great friendship.

"And what about the red one?" Harmony asked.

"It's for *my* heart," John said. "And I'm giving it to you."

Harmony's mouth dropped open and she was speechless.

"I've got to go now. I just wanted to tell you that."

He stood up, shook her hand, went and told Mr. Wilkes good-bye, and then he left. Harmony was blown away. She kicked off her shoes and ran upstairs to call Asia and tell her what just happened.

"Are you serious?" Asia asked.

"Yeah girl. He was so smooth and everything."

"I think someone's in love with you, Harmony."

"Nah. You think so?"

"Duh! He told you what the red rose meant."

"But, what do I say to him?"

"Do you feel the same way?" Asia asked.

"I dunno. We've only been going out for six months."

"Think about it and search your heart. Shoot, pray about it and see what God says."

"I will." Harmony added. Changing the subject, Harmony asked, "Are you getting ready yet, Asia?"

"Nah, girl. My mom told me to wait for her. You know how she is when it's time to go somewhere. It'll take her two hours longer than it takes me. I'm just biding my time."

They laughed because it was true.

"Is your dad coming?" Harmony asked.

"Girl, he's supposed to be there. *And* he's bringin' the new friend-wife with him. I think I'm gonna need you to referee today."

"Okay girl. I got yo' back. Me and Rick will stand on either sides of them. Gotta go now. Jacob's supposed to have the results to the DNA test in an hour."

"Okay, well, call me when you hear," Asia said.

"I will. Bye."

The entire family was on pins and needles waiting to see if Jacob was going to be a father. When Jacob came in he called everyone to the living room.

"Where's the envelope, Jacob?" Mr. Wilkes asked.

"I don't need an envelope. The baby isn't mine."

"How do you know?" Mrs. Wilkes asked.

"LaTonya told me that it wasn't mine because she was sneaking around on me with this other guy."

"You still don't want a DNA test?" asked Harmony.

"Nah. I was having my quiet time this morning before I went to pick LaTonya up to get the results of the test. I was angry and worried. So I opened up my Bible to Psalm 37 and read verses 1 through 9, and that gave me my answer. When I got to LaTonya's house, she opened the door and shouted, "It's not yours!"

"What?" I asked.

"It's not your baby Jacob!"

"La Tonya was seeing this guy named Charles on the side. When she and I were together she always made sure I wore a condom, but she didn't do that with Charles because she wanted to have his child. At first, I was hurt and angry, but the Lord reminded me of the scripture I had just read. I told LaTonya that I was sorry that she felt like I wasn't enough, but that God always has a plan, and it wasn't in His plan for me to become a father right now. I told her to be happy and God bless her. Then I left.

I cried in the car for several reasons. One, because I really loved her; two, because I was trying to picture myself as a father, and three, God had delivered me from certain drama. That's the best part of all."

The family drew in to give Jacob a big group hug and then said a prayer. Mrs. Wilkes decided to go to Asia's graduation with Harmony. Mr. Wilkes and Jacob decided to stay home and have some "man time" together.

After the graduation, Harmony, Asia and Rick dropped Mrs. Wilkes off at home so she could rest. Then, the three musketeers went to have dinner. They went to an Italian restaurant called Ma Bella's. Next to Mrs. Wilkes, they served the best spaghetti and garlic bread in the area. While they were there, she ran into John and his friends, Charles and James. When he saw her he stood up and grinned from ear to ear. He greeted her with a handshake and a hug.

"What are you doing here?" John asked.

"We're here celebrating Asia's graduation."

Harmony said hello to the other men.

"Excuse my manners. Charles, James, this is Harmony, my co-worker."

They both stayed seated and said hello.

"Well, I'll leave you guys to your dinner. John, call me later, okay? I've got something to tell you."

"Will do." He said.

Immediately after she left, John's friends said, "Man, she doesn't look like any co-worker I've ever worked with."

"It's not like that, guys. We're talking, but it's nothing serious."

John hated to downplay his relationship with Harmony, but James and Charles always teased him for being a "Preacher's Kid" and about becoming a preacher. They called him a "PK" every chance they got. He wasn't sure how they'd act if they knew he was in-love with her.

When Harmony returned to her seat, she told Asia and Rick who she had seen. Rick wanted to know some gossip, but there wasn't any to tell. After dinner, they all moved to the dance floor to work off the food they had eaten. Rick and Asia were dancing like little monkeys, while Harmony danced sitting on the stool at the bar. She wasn't much for dancing, unless she had the right partner, and to her, that was John. And he'd already left with his friends.

It was getting late and Harmony wanted to go and check on her mother. If the truth be told, she also wanted to check to see if John had called. They left the restaurant and Harmony dropped everyone off. On her way home, she thought of what John had told her when he handed her the roses. Was he serious? They'd only been seeing each other for six months. Could he possibly fall in love with her in that short of time?

Upon arriving home, Harmony said a quick prayer before stepping out of the car. "Lord, I know you are the Almighty God and you can do anything that you want, but I'm not sure if I feel the same way about John that he does about me. We have been spending a lot of quality time together, but I'm just not sure. Can you point me in the right direction, please? I need your help right now. Amen."

Just then Harmony's phone rang. Grandma Sutton was calling.

"Hello?" Harmony answered.

"Hi. Harmony?"

"Yes, who's this?"

"This is John's grandmother, Maddie."

"Oh. Hi. How are you?"

"Fine. Uh, Harmony, I have something to tell you."

"What is it?" She asked.

"Harmony, John's been in a terrible accident."

"What!?" She screamed.

"Yes, he's over at Memorial Hospital right now and he's asking for you. Can you come right away?"

"Yes, Grandma Maddie. I'll be right there."

Before Harmony left for the hospital she ran into the house to let her parents know what happened and about John's request for her to come. Mr. Wilkes and Jacob decided to go with her to the hospital. They knew that this would take Harmony back to when Tony was killed and they didn't want her driving alone. Jacob drove Harmony's car and Mr. Wilkes and Harmony prayed together while he drove. When they arrived at the hospital, Mr. and Mrs. Sutton were there and so were John's grandparents. The look on their faces made Harmony feel anxious.

"He's in bed eight Harmony." Grandma Maddie said.

Harmony started to go to John's bed and John's mother tried to stop her.

"Sit down Meredith!" Mr. Sutton said.

Harmony kept walking. She then paused before going behind the curtain. She wasn't sure what she would find. Pulling the curtain aside she could see John's eyes were closed and his breathing was labored. He was hooked up to at least three machines. All she heard were beeps and whoosh noises. She put her hand on his hand.

"John, are you okay?"

He opened his eyes and smiled at her.

"I am now," he said.

"What happened?"

"Well, Charles, James and I were just driving around talking in the car on the freeway and this car came from out of nowhere and clipped the back end. Our car just started spinning out of control and all I could do was pray. Harmony, it's true what they say about seeing your life flash before your eyes. And in my pictures, I saw my family, friends and you."

While John was talking, the nurse came in and said they had to take him into surgery.

"What's wrong with him?" Harmony asked.

"He has a few broken ribs; that's why his breath is short and there's a little swelling on his brain. The doctor needs to relieve the pressure."

"Harmony?" John called out.

"Yes John?"

"Will you marry me?"

"What did you say?" She asked.

"Ma'am," the nurse said, "he's not thinking clearly."

"John, what did you say?" asked Harmony.

"Will you marry me? Answer me now."

Harmony thought he was out of his mind and wouldn't remember what she said.

"Uh, yes, John. Yes. I'll marry you."

"Ma'am, we have to take him now."

John squeezed her hand and told her that he'd see her later. When Harmony got back to the waiting room, everyone asked her what had happened.

"They're taking him into surgery. He should be out in a few hours. Daddy? Harmony asked. "Can we go to the chapel?"

"Yes Princess. Let's go."

What should have been a few hours of surgery turned into seven hours. None of the doctors or nurses gave the family any information about what was going on. All Harmony could do was think back to when Tony was killed. She had a hard time staying focused while sitting in the waiting room. All of this was still too familiar. She looked over at Mrs. Sutton, John's mother, and decided to go over to talk to her. As Harmony approached her, she decided to say a silent prayer.

"Mrs. Sutton?"

"Yes?"

"You know, John's a strong man. He'll be fine."

Harmony was not only trying to calm Mrs. Sutton down, but to convince herself of it as well. She knew who God was, but she was afraid of what could happen to John. Harmony sat down beside her and gently reached for her hand. At first, Mrs. Sutton pulled away, but then she could feel the sincerity that flowed from Harmony's heart and she grabbed her hand and squeezed it. Mr. Sutton came back from getting some coffee and saw the two of them sitting together.

"Praise the Lord," he said under his breath.

Finally, Dr. Montes came to the waiting room to give them an update.

"John had more bleeding on the brain than he thought, and he had a broken leg along with the broken ribs. One of John's ribs punctured his lung. They were able to set his leg and wrap his chest. The bleeding took the longest, but it has stopped as well. John still has a lot of swelling on his brain. It was out of their hands now. We'll have to wait to see what morning brings."

"Dr. Montes?" Mr. Sutton asked.

"Yes?"

"What can we expect when John comes out of it?"

"Well, *if* he comes out of it, he could have some brain damage. But, we won't know anything until morning. The next 12 hours are critical."

"What about the other men in the car?"

"Charles made it, but James didn't. He was bleeding so much that we couldn't do anything for him. Their families have been called."

"Thank you, doctor." Mr. Sutton said.

When the doctor left, everyone had their heads hung low. Some were hung low out of fear and some were hung low out of just plain old sadness. Harmony decided to leave and go check on her mom at home. She told Mr. and Mrs. Sutton that she'd be back later and not to worry. Jacob, Harmony and Mr. Wilkes were headed for the door when Mrs. Sutton called out to Harmony. Harmony turned around to find her standing directly in her face.

"Thank you." Mrs. Sutton said.

Then, Mrs. Sutton gave Harmony a big hug. Harmony and her family just smiled and left the room. On the drive home, Jacob pointed out how well Harmony and Mrs. Sutton were getting along.

"Maybe it's just because of what's going on." Harmony said.

"People tend to come together in times like these," Mr. Wilkes added.

Harmony just sat quietly, listening.

After checking on Mrs. Wilkes, Harmony drove back to the hospital to check on John. His family had gone home. She went into his room and sat at his bedside. He looked so helpless, but cute at the same time. While sitting next to him she held John's hand. His hands were rough and his fingers were thick. His hands were also well-manicured. It was odd to Harmony that his hands looked as if he'd been working outside all his life, but this was his first job. She then began to pray over him.

"Lord, you are the creator of everything good. This is a good man. He's got so much to do for you and in ministry. He's been really good to me and my family and to his own family. I'm asking for you to come in and heal his body perfectly so that he can continue to do Your work. I guess I have an interest in him too. But it's more for You and Your ministry. Lord, he asked me to marry him. I only said 'yes' because I thought he was out of his head. But I feel a genuine connection to him, especially now. Let your will be done. Please! I really care for him and I don't want to lose him. I know it's not about me, but…,"

Just then, Harmony started to cry. While she was crying she felt John squeeze her hand.

"What are you doing here?" he whispered. "I thought we were just colleagues in the fight."

Surprised, she raised her head and gave him a hug.

"Oh John, you're awake!"

"Ow! Uh, yeah. Why wouldn't I wake up?" he asked.

"The doctor said that *if* you woke up, you might have brain damage."

"Well, I do feel like I got hit by a train. Harmony? Where are James and Charles?"

"I'll get the doctor." She said.

When Dr. Montes came in, he checked John's vital signs. Dr. Montes asked Harmony to leave the room while he checked John thoroughly. When she came back in, John was crying.

"What happened?" She asked the doctor.

"I had to tell him about his friend. John's going to be fine, physically."

"Thank you, doctor." Harmony said.

Harmony immediately ran to his side and climbed into the bed. She lay next to him to comfort him. Dr. Montes left the room. She knew exactly what John was feeling. He cried for what seemed like an hour. All she did was lay there holding him. John wouldn't let Harmony leave his side, not even to call his family to tell them he was awake.

John finally fell asleep. He was lying in Harmony's arms when she remembered to call his family. She gently left his side, called his parents and hers; they arrived quickly. When she tried to leave to give his family some time with him, John called out to her.

"Harmony?"

"Yes?" She answered.

"Thank you."

"You're welcome."

Mr. and Mrs. Sutton were overjoyed when they saw him talking. They knew that it was only by the grace of God that he was not only alive, but that he didn't have any brain damage.

"Mom, Dad," John said.

"Yes son?"

"I'm in love with that girl. I'm in love with Harmony. Now Mom, I know she's not the one you wanted, but it's not about you. God has shown me who she is to me."

Mrs. Sutton sat, pursing her lips.

"While I was sleeping I had a dream. And in this dream it was me, Harmony and our families. We were having a party or something. When I looked around to get a good look at what was going on, I saw that we were at a wedding. It was *our* wedding; Me and Harmony's. And at the head of the room was a man dressed in white. I looked at him and he just nodded to me. I looked around to see if it was me he was looking at and he did it again. He nodded to me. I went up to him and asked him why he was nodding. The first thing he said was, "Turn around." I turned around and Harmony was standing there in a wedding gown waiting for me at the door. She was so beautiful, Dad. She had this light around her that was indescribable. Then the man dressed in white told me something. He told me to "go and get her right now." As I walked towards her, the light got brighter and brighter. Then I woke up and Harmony was right here sitting at my bedside crying."

"Son, calm down." Mr. Sutton said.

"What did the doctor say, John?" Mrs. Sutton asked.

"He told me that I would be fine and that I still had to be careful with my leg. And that I couldn't do any heavy lifting because of my ribs. John began to cough. I'm not supposed to be talking so much because of my lung. He also told me what happened with James and Charles, and that James didn't survive the accident."

"Oh Lord, his mother must be going out of her mind right now." Mrs. Sutton said.

"Mom, can you go by there and see if she needs anything?" John asked.

"Yeah, baby. I'll do that."

"Okay, Meredith. Let's let him get some sleep."

"Mom, could you ask Harmony to come back in please?" Rolling her eyes, she said, "Yes, I'll get her for you."

Harmony came back into the room to see what John wanted. He told her to go home and get some rest. And he thanked her again for being there for him.

"That's what a friend is for." She said.

"Oh no! We're not just friends anymore, remember? You said 'yes' to my proposal."

She thought he wouldn't remember, but he did.

"Oh yeah. Now I remember. I thought you were just talking out of your head." They laughed and Harmony, changing the subject, told him that she would see him later.

It had been two weeks and John was at home recovering, not only from his accident, but also from the funeral for James. John hadn't talked to Charles personally yet, but Mrs. Sutton had checked on him and gave John a good report. Charles had a small head injury and his arm was broken, but he would fully recover.

Harmony had gone back to work and found that Callie and Shondra kept things running smoothly for her while she was away. Ron and Danny put in a lot of overtime as well. While John was away, Mr. Langston asked Harmony to be interim Vice-President. She gladly accepted the job.

Harmony called Callie into her office.

"I want to thank you for holding down the fort while we were away."

"You sure put in a lot of time at the hospital boss lady for somebody that's *only* a co-worker." Callie said.

"Yeah, you're right. John, um Mr. Sutton will be fine. He'll still be out for a couple of weeks though, until he can walk on his crutches better. Callie, do you remember me talking to you about keeping your business, your business?" Harmony asked.

"Yeah, boss lady. Why?"

"Well, I need you to keep my business, my business. Is that clear?"

"Yes, Ms. Wilkes. Crystal clear."

"Thank you," Harmony said. "You've done a fine job and I'm proud of you." Callie just walked out of the office giggling and went back to work.

Another two weeks passed and it was Sunday morning. Harmony went to church with John and his family since it was his first week back. Harmony sat with John's family. The congregation was smiling at her. She didn't know if it was out of joy or fear because they knew how Mrs. Sutton was about her son, John. Pastor Sutton talked about getting right with God and to stop playing games. During the invitation a few people came down the aisle.

One girl came down the aisle asking for prayer for her family's finances. Then, another young woman stood up and started talking. Her voice was very familiar, but Harmony couldn't see who it was. When she finally got a good glance, she saw that it was Callie from work. Callie had come down to re-dedicate her life to Christ and to ask for prayer for the father of her children.

"He's going through some hard-core stuff right now. These are my two children, Jaylyn and Christopher."

The congregation prayed with her and then a counselor took her in the back to get all of her information. Just as Pastor Sutton turned around to go back to the pulpit, a man came down the aisle and cried out.

"Help me!" Pastor Sutton turned back to face him.

"What can I do for you, young man?"

"My name is Charles and I need to give my life to the Lord. And I need to do it now!"

"Son?" Pastor Sutton asked. "Why do you want to do that?"

"Because I was raised in the church and I know better. I know that it's better to be in than to be out."

"Do you know who Jesus is?" Pastor Sutton asked.

"A little, but I would like to know a lot." Charles answered.

Pastor Sutton did the sinners prayer with him and then asked if he was willing to get baptized as well.

"Yes!" Charles answered excitedly.

The entire congregation cheered, and Harmony stood up and clapped.

"I need to say something." Charles said.

Pastor Sutton gave him the microphone to speak.

"The woman that came down before me is the mother of two of my children. I'm the man she's talking about. I'm the father of her kids. See, my friends, James and John and I were in a car accident about four weeks ago. James didn't make it. But John and I did. While I was hurting in that hospital, all I could think of were my children and the mothers of my children. And how I was accusing Callie of doing wrong when all along, it was me. I told her that the woman I was seeing, LaTonya, was only a friend, but she was more than that. Now LaTonya is pregnant with one of my children. I want to say I'm sorry to the Lord, to the congregation, and to Callie. I don't know if she'll take me back and I won't blame her if she doesn't, but I just know that right now, I gotta get my life in order or else."

"We'll accept you on your statement, Charles." Pastor Sutton said.

A male counselor took him in the back to get his information. Right before Pastor Sutton had the people to stand for the benediction, he said that John Jr. wanted to say something. John stood up to speak to the congregation.

"Thank you for your prayers, cards and letters. Without them, I wouldn't have recovered as fast as I did. While I was in the hospital, before surgery, I had a long talk with a friend. Her name is Harmony. Harmony, could you stand?" he asked.

Harmony stood up and the congregation gasped.

"Harmony and I have been friends for about a year or more now. We started off as colleagues and then we started to take a liking to one another. It's only been a little over six months since we became serious about each other. I've found that we have a lot in common. But most of all we both love the Lord. For quite some time now, I have noticed that I can't stand to be away from her. I think about her all the time. I respect her as a woman of God, and as a person. And just a little over a month ago, I gave her my heart."

John came from around the podium so that the congregation could see him completely. John motioned to his father to help him down.

"While I was in the hospital, the Lord showed me that Harmony was the one and He told me to go and get her right now." When I woke up, Harmony was sitting at my bedside holding my hand and crying."

John, feeling a little bit of pain, got down on one knee.

"Harmony, before my surgery I asked you a question. Do you remember what it was?"

"Yes." She replied while shaking. "But your head was messed up then."

"My head wasn't messed up then and it isn't messed up now. The Lord showed me in a dream that you were the one. And if you trust Him with your life and me with your heart, can you please answer the same way that you did then? Harmony Michelle Wilkes, I ask you again, will you marry me?"

She stood frozen with her mouth open and tears in her eyes. Harmony looked down at Mrs. Sutton and Grandma Maddie. Then she looked around and saw Jacob, Asia, Rick and her mom and dad in the back. They all nodded their heads in agreement. Harmony looked up.

"Yes John. Yes, I'll marry you."

She made her way to the aisle, knelt down and hugged him. The congregation cheered and laughed. There were a few women who were sad because they thought it would be them whom he would marry. While everyone was in a good mood, Pastor Sutton had everyone to stand and gave the benediction.

After church, the people came up to congratulate them on their engagement. Harmony's head was swimming. She was overwhelmed. She couldn't believe that everyone knew, except her.

"He made us keep it a secret sis," Jacob said.

Harmony hugged them all, and felt so much joy in her heart. Both families went out to dinner to celebrate. Mrs. Sutton made sure that they knew everyone paid for their own meal. Grandpa Rufus told Mrs. Sutton to chill out and just enjoy the day. Callie and Harmony talked when the crowd moved away from them.

"I'm proud of you," Harmony said.

"Thanks."

"So, the very Charles you were telling me about was the same guy that was John's best friend?"

"Yeah, but I didn't know they were best friends. He never talked about him by name. He just called him 'his boy.'"

"What are you going to do now?" Harmony asked.

"Well, I'm going to get involved in the church. And make sure my kids do too. As far as Charles and the other woman carrying his child go, I'll let the Lord handle that. But whatever He decides, Callie pointing in the air, I'll be fine with."

"Hey, you want to come to dinner with us?" Harmony asked.

"Can the kids come too?"

"Yes the kids can come."

"You buying boss lady?"

"Yeah, I'm buying," Harmony said laughing.

"Then we'll come."

"Let's go. You can ride with me and my fiancée."

They laughed, got into the car and drove away.

Chapter Eight

GETTING TO KNOW YOU

ONDAY CAME TOO soon for all of them. It was back to business as usual. The office was buzzing about the ring on Harmony's ring finger, although no one actually said anything out loud. Each of them went to Callie and Shondra to see what *they* knew.

"Come on, Callie," Danny said. "I know you know something."

"Look." Callie said, "Leave her alone. It's probably a fake anyways."

Callie decided to sit down for a minute and say a quick prayer.

"Thank you, Lord for holding my tongue. Harmony trusts me and I'd like to keep it that way. And I'd like to be a woman of God just like her. Please direct me. Amen."

Harmony went into John's office to speak with him privately. Just because she is his fiancée now doesn't mean she has privileges in the office. It does, but she didn't want the team members knowing anything. She knocked as she always did and entered upon his request. She closed the door behind her. When he looked up she gave him a huge grin. He walked over to her and gave her a hug. They were glad to see each other. But then they both remembered to use handshakes not hugs. They discussed business first then a wedding date.

"Well," Harmony said. "I'd like to have a long engagement."

"How long?" John asked.

"At least 1½ to two years," she said.

"What? That's too long!" John said.

"No it's not. That gives us time to get to know each other better, and plan an elegant ceremony. Plus, I'd like to know that Ma's out of the woods before we move ahead. And…" Harmony said.

"And what?" John asked.

"I'd like to apply for another job."

John leaned back in his chair and said, "What other job, Harmony?"

"Well, Mr. Langston approached me last week about working upstairs in the public relations department."

"And when were you going to tell me about this?" John asked.

"My plan was to tell you this week. You caught me off guard at church yesterday. And I wasn't going to discuss it in front of our families. John, it pays $15,000 more a year and I get to travel three times a year, with pay. And it won't be so awkward with us working in the same department. We don't have to pretend anymore. And I don't want anyone thinking that you helped me get to where I am, because I'm in love with you."

John came from around his desk.

"What did you say?" he asked.

"I said that I didn't want things to be awkward with us in the same office. And I don't have to hide the fact that we're engaged."

"No, you said something else. You used the words 'in-love.'"

She smiled and said, "Yes, I did say that."

"Are you in-love with me Harmony Michelle Wilkes?"

"Yes, John. I am." He leaned in to give her a kiss, but she backed away.

"Not until our wedding day." She insisted with a grin.

"Ah, come on!" John said. "Are you serious?"

"Yes, I am." She gave him a Holy hug and a handshake, then told him she'd talk to him later about taking the new position. Let's meet at Ma Bella's for lunch."

Remembering what happened the last time they were there, John said, "No. Let's meet at Carol's Diner over on Third and Main."

She agreed, blew him a kiss, and turned and walked out of his office. John sat back down at his desk and looked up at the ceiling and said, "Lord, I need your help now! I don't know if I can wait two years to be with her."

Just then the phone rang. It was his father. As John said hello, his dad was already talking to someone else in the background.

"Hold on, it won't be long before you get what you want. If you don't wait for me, you'll regret it." Mr. Sutton said.

"What did you say, Dad?"

"Oh, I was talking to your mother. She wants to spend my money and not tell me why and on what."

"Oh," John said. He was thinking about what he had just asked the Lord about. "What's up, Dad?"

"Son, your grandparents want you and Harmony over for dinner sometime this week. They want to grill her about her family."

"Why?" John asked.

"You know how women are."

"But Grandma Maddie loves Harmony."

"Well, that was before the proposal. I'll make sure they don't plan a hangin'. We'll all be together for the entire night."

"Are you sure?" John asked.

"Yeah, I'll make sure of it. You'd better clue Harmony in on everything so she can be prepared."

"Okay, I will Dad."

"I have to go now, son."

"Okay. Bye Dad."

At lunch with Harmony, John told Harmony about the phone call from his father, and what to prepare for. Harmony was not surprised when he told her. She actually expected it.

"Really?" John asked.

"Yeah. Me and Asia were talking earlier about your family and she was saying that it's a wonder they haven't grilled me yet."

They both laughed and continued talking.

"So, John said. "Where do you get your name from?"

"Well," Harmony said, "my Dad was a huge music buff back in the day. He used to be in a jazz band when he and my mother were dating. After they were married and my mother was pregnant with Jacob and then with me, my mom would go hear him play. My mother said I would stretch every time my dad would play his saxophone or sing with the guys. But the only time I'd jump in my mom's belly was when they would sing in harmony. If there was someone singing a solo I wouldn't move at all. So when I was born, my dad said, "we'll call her Harmony." Ma really liked the name. Jacob thought it was dumb, but he is a boy so…It makes sense because my mom's name is Belle. You already know my favorite color is baby blue. I was born on a Monday morning. Maybe that's why I love the day time. Kind of corny huh?"

"No. It's not corny."

"Anything else you'd like to know?" Harmony asked.

"Yes, what color do you want for our wedding?" John asked.

"Well, what is your favorite color?" she asked.

"I like blue too. But I'm more on the cooler blue side. Like the darker blues."

"Well, we could use them both."

"Okay, then both it is." John agreed.

"We don't have a date yet." Harmony said.

"How about we get married in late winter in *two* years?" John asked. "The cool blue would be nice that time of year."

"Exactly what month are you talking about, because there are three of them?"

"I like February 14," John said.

"Why *that* date?" Harmony asked.

"That's the day exactly ten years ago when I got my calling to preach."

"But what about Valentine's Day? I'm not sharing that day." Harmony stated.

"Well, how about the following Saturday, the 21st?" John asked. "I'll just have to buy you two gifts."

"You'd better," she said. "Okay, February 21st works for me. Do you think it will be odd to have the color blue in that month?"

"Who cares!" John replied. "We're different!"

"Yes we are!" Said Harmony.

Their food arrived and it looked delicious. They both ordered the salmon with fresh vegetables and a small salad. They took their time eating because they were the boss.

"When are we going to have dinner with your family?" Harmony asked.

"My mother suggested Thursday night at 6:30." John replied.

"Okay, but I have a meeting that evening with Mr. Langston at 5:30 about the job he offered me. I'll come by right after it's over."

"Do I get any say so on you taking this new job?" John asked.

"Of course you do. What do you think about me taking the new job?"

"Is it something you want? Will it take away from our relationship and us spending time together? What are your hours like?"

"Hey, hold on!" she said. "Let me answer the first one. Okay, here goes. Yes, I want it. Yes, it will take away from us and enhance us too, but I promise to make sure we get plenty of quality time. I will be working the same hours as I do now. The only extra thing I will be doing is traveling four times a year."

"Whoa! I thought you said three?"

"I'm kididng," Harmony said. "It's three."

When lunch was over, they left at different times so that no one would suspect anything when they got back to the office.

Upon arriving, John heard his name.

"Mr. Sutton?" his secretary called out.

"Yes?"

"You have a call on line two. It's Mr. Langston."

"Thank you." John went into his office and took the call. "Mr. Langston, good afternoon. How are you?"

"Fine, John. I have a few questions to ask you about Ms. Wilkes."

"Yes Sir?"

"How efficient is she in her job?"

"Well, without sounding like I'm biased, she's excellent! She's very thorough. She triple checks all of her work and her team's work. When I get the files from her during the day I don't have to be concerned about her quality of work."

"What about her work ethics?" Mr. Langston asked.

"Harmony does not allow any excuses for why something can't be done. And why it's not done on time. She keeps the lines of communication open with me and her team. She lets them know up front that she won't take a bullet for anyone in this job for laziness, cheating, stealing or anything else that's against company policy, even if you took a pencil from your desk. Her integrity is top notch! She's a rare gem Sir!"

"Thank you, John. That helps me tremendously."

"You're welcome, sir."

John hung up the phone and got back to work. Now he had to just sit and wait to see what would happen with the possibility of a new job for Harmony.

During the week, Callie, Harmony, Danny and Ron had lunch together. They were discussing new strategies for the company. Shondra opted to stay at the office. She still wasn't one of Harmony's biggest fans. Plus, she was feeling lonely. They didn't know it, but Harmony was sizing them all up to see who she could recommend to Mr. Langston to take her place in the event that she got the promotion. They were all good candidates. They had been well-trained. She would miss them, she thought.

It was Wednesday and Harmony was at home with her father discussing the upcoming big dinner at John's grandparents' house.

"Well, Princess, all you can do is be yourself, nothing more," Mr. Wilkes said.

"I don't know why you need to prove yourself to those snobby people." Jacob said.

"You know how some people are, even people in the church. Jesus, Himself, ate with sinners." Harmony said.

"She'll be fine." Mrs. Wilkes said.

"Thanks Ma."

As Harmony headed upstairs, they all said, "Say a prayer before you go." Then they laughed because they were all in 'harmony' with one another. Harmony went upstairs to call Asia and Rick on three-way.

"I think you should make them all kick rocks!" Rick said.

"Shut up!" Asia interjected. "These are going to be her in-laws pretty soon. She can't kick 'em to the curb."

"But, she can make them mind their own business." Rick said.

"It makes sense for them to want to get to know her better. All they'll do is size her up by asking how much, how old, are you or not and how come."

"What?" Harmony asked.

"Money, age, virginity and marrying John."

"Oh!" Rick and Harmony said together.

"Well, I have answers for all of them."

"You'll be fine. Just pray first." Asia and Rick said.

"I will." Harmony said. "Thanks, guys. Gotta go now. I'll call y'all later."

"Good night." Rick and Asia said.

After Harmony hung up the phone she spent some time in prayer with the Lord. While praying, she fell asleep and woke up to her alarm clock the next morning.

At work, Harmony was working extra fast. All she had on her mind was the interview with Mr. Langston and John's family. She didn't even go into his office to say good morning. She did send John an e-mail saying hi and that she loved him and that she would be very busy today, and to forgive her for not coming to see him. John's reply was "I love you too, Michelle. Go get 'em!" She smiled and kept moving along.

The meeting with Mr. Langston went well. He asked her all of the same questions that he had asked John earlier in the week, plus a few more. He asked about where she grew up, her home life and her future goals. The conversation was very laid-back and short. Mr. Langston asked Harmony if there was anyone that she could think of that could take her place and do just as good a job as she did as the Quality Control Engineer.

"Yes!" she replied. "I think Callie Johnson would be a great candidate for the job. In the last year she has come through for the team on more than a few occasions. She's always on time and critiques everything she does to make sure it is worthy of our approval."

"Thank you, Ms. Wilkes, for your time." Mr. Langston said. "You'll be hearing from me one way or the other about the job in about a week."

"Thank you, Mr. Langston, for the opportunity," Harmony said.

She shook his hand and said good night. Harmony left with just enough time to meet with John's family and not be late. They arrived at the same time at John's grandparents' house and greeted one another with a hug and a handshake.

"I missed you today." Harmony said to John.

"I missed you too." He replied. "How was the interview with Mr. Langston?"

"I think it went well. He said I'd hear from him in about a week."

"Do you feel good about it?" he asked.

"Yes I do," Harmony said.

"Good."

They rang the doorbell and Grandma Maddie answered the door. She greeted them with hugs and kisses.

"Come in!" Grandma Maddie said.

She took their coats and told them to have a seat.

"John, can you come into the kitchen and help me?" Grandma Maddie asked. "But, wash your hands first."

"Yes ma'am."

While John was in the kitchen, Grandpa Rufus came into the living room and began to grill Harmony. At some point, Grandpa Rufus asked Harmony how much money she made.

"I make a pretty good living, Sir." Harmony said.

That answer did not please Grandpa Rufus. He got up and walked into the kitchen. Soon afterward, John came back into the living room to speak with Harmony.

"What happened?" John asked.

"I dunno. He asked me how much money I made and I gave him an adequate answer."

"Uh-oh. That means you didn't tell him what he wanted to hear, right?"

"Yeah, I guess. Why?" Harmony asked.

"Well, now they think you've got something to hide."

Mrs. Sutton, John's mother, entered the room.

"Harmony dear, would you like something to drink?"

"Water, with no ice, would be fine, thanks."

"No dear, I meant would you like a *drink?*"

Harmony, looking surprised at her, said, "No thank you. I don't drink."

Thinking about what was just asked of her, Harmony pondered, aren't they Christians?

John saw the puzzled look on her face and in a denying tone he immediately said, "That's them, not me."

Dinner was ready and Pastor Sutton called everyone to the table. He asked John Jr. to bless the food. They all held hands and prayed. After the prayer John's family began discussing community and world events. The conversation was evenly spread at the table, and everyone seemed to be comfortable with one another. That was until Harmony's cell phone rang. John's mother got angry.

"No phones at the table dear."

"I'm sorry. I have to take this. It's my mother."

Harmony got up from the table and went into the other room to talk to her mom.

"How are things going?" Mrs. Wilkes asked.

"It's okay Ma, but I have to call you back later. They don't like us on the phone during dinner."

"Excuse me?" Mrs. Wilkes asked.

"I'll call you later, Ma."

"Love you baby. Daddy says hi too."

"Okay, love him too. Bye."

When Harmony returned to the table everyone was staring at her except John. He was shoving food in his mouth with his head down.

"Is everything okay dear?" Mrs. Sutton asked.

"Yes. Thank you. Please accept my apologies everyone."

"John?" Mrs. Sutton asked, "How are things at work?"

"Fine, Mom."

Grandma Maddie asked Harmony if her cell phone would be going off any more tonight.

Respectfully and surprisingly Harmony replied, "No, Grandma Maddie, it won't." Harmony then turned her phone off.

After dinner, everyone went into the living room for coffee, except Nettie. Nettie wanted to go upstairs and talk on the phone about all the drama that was going on at her house. Nettie said good night to everyone and gave Harmony a big hug. She then told Harmony how cool it was going to be to have a big sister. They just smiled at one another and Nettie went upstairs. John's mother was not pleased with what she heard Nettie say. John's father began talking about a wedding date.

"We're going to have a long engagement." John Jr. stated.

"Why?" John's mother asked.

"Because it will give us time to get to know one another and our families a little better. Plus, Harmony is changing jobs. And this job will have her traveling a lot."

"What?" said Grandpa Rufus in shock!

"I'll only be traveling three times a year and I'll make sure John and I get enough quality time in between."

"Son, I don't think you need to be marrying a woman that's not going to put her family first." Pastor Sutton demanded.

"What about the kids?" Mrs. Sutton asked.

"What kids?" asked Harmony. "We've only been engaged for four days."

"You mean you don't want kids?" asked Meredith snobbishly.

"Wait, wait, wait!" John shouted. "Mother, Harmony and I are in agreement with waiting two years to get married. I'm fine with the new job. I trust her to do what she says she will do. End of discussion."

Grandma Maddie, Grandpa Rufus and Pastor Sutton closed their mouths immediately. Meredith was sitting down looking offended, but she knew that at this moment she had no voice.

"Harmony, are you ready for me to walk you to your car?" John asked.

"Yes John. Thank you. It was a lovely dinner." Harmony said sarcastically. "Good night everyone."

And in a mumbling tone, they all said good night. As John and Harmony stood at the car, they just looked into each other's eyes. It was blue black outside, and the two of them could only see the whites of one another's eyes. His were shining in the night from the full moon. She got lost in them and laid her head on his shoulder. He held her for a while then he knew he had to let her go because of two reasons. The first reason was because she had a long drive. The second reason was because he desired to kiss her in the moonlight. He thought she looked absolutely beautiful. Sensing the yearning between them they pulled away from each other and shook hands. John opened her car door.

"Please drive carefully, and call me when you get home."

"I will." She said.

At the thought of him being such a gentleman she smiled.

He watched her drive off. When John turned back to the house he saw his family standing in the window watching them.

"That boy's in-love Meredith." Grandma Maddie said as she looked at John's mother.

"Yep!" Grandpa Rufus added.

John's mother closed the drapes and sat down on the couch. She then began to cry.

"Oh Lord. Here we go," said Pastor Sutton.

Chapter Nine

Sharing Is Caring/
Boys For Life

A<small>FTER THE EXCITING</small> evening with John's family, John decided that it was time for the groomsmen to hang out a little more. John was not only preparing for marriage, but starting a new, part-time job and attend seminary full-time. He wanted to make sure that all the guys were well-acquainted with one another. Jacob, Charles and John decided to meet off and on for the next six to eight months. They met at Jacob's house most of the time. Because of this, this time, they decided to go Charles' apartment and shoot some hoops for a while.

"Man, I'm excited about leaving United Aerospace to attend seminary. I will miss the hustle of the job, but I'll be fine. I won't get to see my lady during the day like I used to though."

"Man," Jacob said, "What are they going to do about replacing you?"

"I'm not sure." John said. "Mr. Langston is looking for a replacement now."

"Oh really?" Jacob asked.

"Why are you so interested in it anyway? You've got a nice cushy job over at Metler's Engineering."

Jacob got very quiet. John and Charles looked up him and both said, "What?"

"Metler's is filing Chapter 11." Jacob said.

"What?!" They both exclaimed.

"Yeah, I figured I wouldn't tell anyone yet. I had to pray about it first. I know that the Lord will make a way."

"Hey Jacob, you want me to talk to Mr. Langston for you?"

"Yeah, I would appreciate that," Jacob said.

"What kind of degree do you have?"

"I have my Masters in Engineering. I've been in an upper management position for 3 years now. I've wanted to move up, but the CEO wants to keep family on hand to be in charge. And now that they're filing bankruptcy, my position is one of the first to go."

"When is your last day?" Charles asked.

"I have three months left."

"Dang!" both Charles and John said at the same time.

"Okay Jacob, I'll talk to Mr. Langston later this afternoon. He doesn't usually take interviews over the phone, but since I've been with him for so long and he loves your sister, maybe he'll take this one."

"Thanks, John." Jacob said. "Anything at this point can only help. But don't tell my folks, or my bossy little sister."

"Alright man, I won't say anything."

"So Charles, how are things with Callie?" John asked.

"They're okay man. I'm just trying to survive out here. You know, I wanna take care of my kids first before thinking about getting back with her. Callie's a good woman and if God means for us to be together, then it will happen. If not, then I'm okay with that too. My business is thriving and I'm healthy, so I'm not worried about anything else at this point."

"What kind of business do you have Charles?" asked Jacob.

"I own a home cleaning service called, 'Sho-Nuff' Clean; Just like Mama Used To Do It.' It's located in the Downtown Square. I only work for the upscale folks of this city. I'm the youngest of six. I have five older sisters. Yeah, the boys in the neighborhood, including John, used to make fun of me when I was little. My sisters used to pay me to clean their rooms. And my mother didn't want me to rely on a woman to take care of me, so while my sisters were out chasing boys, I was in the kitchen with momma learning how to cook and clean. And, I must say that I am pretty darn good!"

"What about your other girl?" John asked.

"LaTonya? That was just my 'one-night-stand' girl. Well, actually, more than one night, but you know what I mean. She's pregnant right now, but I don't know if it's mine."

At that moment Jacob looked up at Charles.

"Yeah, she said she was seeing this other dude at some point in our relationship, but she swears it's mine."

"Are you going to have a DNA test?" John asked.

"No. I know it's mine. I was just trying to run from responsibility. I was always her 'go-to guy' when she had a fight with her boyfriend. We were 'friends with benefits', you know? She always made the other guy wear a condom. But I didn't have to. I was 'special'."

"Do you love her?" Jacob asked.

"No, well not like she'd like. She wants us to be a family, but I'm in love with Callie. She's who I should be with."

"So why aren't you with her?" Jacob asked.

"As I said before, I screwed up and I need to get my life together first. Then, if it's in God's will, it will happen."

"So what are you going to do about LaTonya?"

"Nothing. Kick her to the curb, but I will take care of my daughter."

"It's a girl?" John asked.

"Yeah," Charles replied. "After James died and I gave my life to the Lord, I realized that I needed to handle my business with Callie and with her. No more games, man. Callie knows about her, but La Tonya doesn't know about Callie. Anyway, I feel bad for the sucker she was seeing while she was seeing me. La Tonya said he was crying and everything, but he came from a good family. And she said he was too sappy for her."

Just then, Jacob walked over to Charles and punched him in the face.

The Preacher and the Princess

"What was that for man?" Charles asked.

"How could you treat women like that man?"

"Jacob, this ain't got nothin' to do with you," John said.

Jacob, furious, spoke to Charles in a loud voice.

"It has everything to do with me! I'm that sucker you talkin' about!" Jacob shouted.

Charles and John both said, "What?"

"Yeah, I was seeing her for a long time and I thought we were getting closer. I did *everything* for that girl! Whatever she wanted, she got from *me!* She said that I was her one and only lover! I gave up my family time because I didn't want to lose her. She'd always tell me, "what you won't do, someone else will." So I made sure I did it all. Or so I thought. Then she told me that she was pregnant. But I questioned the paternity of the child because sometimes when we had a big fight, she wouldn't call or come over to see me for days at a time. She always took off somewhere overnight. We would get back together later on, but she would never tell me where she went."

"I guess you didn't give her everything because she was with me." Charles said securely.

"Duh! I know that now. Man, that girl hurt me somethin' fierce. Harmony was ready to kick her butt, but I told her that wouldn't be the 'Christian' thing to do."

"I didn't know, Jacob." Charles confessed.

"Look John. I love you like a brother, man, but I'm not going to be in the wedding if he's in it too. You gotta choose."

"What?" John exclaimed. "Man, y'all both my boys. I can't choose."

"Then I will!" Jacob said. "I'm out!"

Jacob slammed the ball down and walked away.

"Jacob!" John called. "Come back, man!"

"Let him go!" Charles said. "I'm the best man anyway." John looked back at him like he wanted to punch him too. He was thinking that he may be a youth minister, but he was still a man. Jacob left in his car, infuriated.

"Man, we can't just let him leave like that. He might have an accident. Let's go after him!" John said.

"You go." Charles said. "He's your boy! I'm going in the house to take a shower."

John was disappointed with Charles for not being a man about this situation. When he got into the car he started thinking out loud.

"Oh Lord, when Harmony finds out, it's gonna get ugly!"

He headed for the Wilkes' home. He wanted to tell Harmony before Jacob got a chance to. On the way there, driving down the freeway, John closed one of his eyes and began to pray.

"Dear Lord, I need your help. Please keep Jacob safe while he's driving upset. And meet me at The Wilkes' house because I need your strength and guidance and much protection from Harmony when she finds out. In Jesus' name, Amen."

John opened his other eye and continued driving.

When John arrived at the Wilkes' place, Jacob's car was nowhere to be found. Where is he? John thought. John said aloud, "nobody but you Lord." Harmony's car was there, so John went up to the door and knocked. Harmony answered the door.

"Hi there." She said.

"Hey girl!" John said in a loud voice.

He shook her hand and went inside. He was breathing hard and sweating.

"What's wrong, John?" She asked.

"Is Jacob here?" John asked.

"No. I thought he was with you and Charles."

"Um, no he left."

"John, why are you acting so weird? And why are you so sweaty?"

John looked up at the ceiling.

"A divine plan I guess." John stated.

"What?" Harmony said. "You're not making any sense."

"Sit down, Michelle." With that Harmony knew something was wrong. He only called her 'Michelle' in serious situations.

"Wait, John. Is your mom still crying?"

"No." He answered. "But I will be soon."

"What? What are you talking about John?"

"Harmony, Jacob and Charles got into it while we were playing basketball."

"What? Why?"

"It was because of LaTonya."

"What about her?"

"Charles is the guy LaTonya was going to for sex while she was dating Jacob. But I didn't know they were with the same girl at the same time."

"Ew!" Harmony said. "Well, you didn't know John."

"Harm, I don't know where Jacob is. He was so furious with Charles when he left."

"Did you call his cell?"

"No. I was too busy praying on the freeway driving over here."

"Okay, well let's pray again." Harmony said.

While they were praying Jacob walked in the door. He was drenched with sweat.

"Where've you been?" Harmony asked.

"Driving and running at the same time?" John questioned.

"No." Jacob said. "I went to the track. I had to think. Look, John, I know you didn't know about me and LaTonya and how Charles fit into it. I'm sorry for what I said, and I'd like to be back in the wedding, if you still want me."

"Of course man, you're about to be my "real" brother."

As John and Jacob were embracing the doorbell rang. It was Charles.

"Hi Charles." Harmony said.

"Hey Harmony. Is Jacob here?"

"Yea, come in."

"Hey man. Can we talk?" Charles asked.

"Yea." Jacob said.

"Look, I'm sorry about the whole thing with LaTonya. I know it wasn't right what we were doing, and at the time I didn't care."

"And, I'm sorry for hitting you," Jacob said.

"I've known John since we were 14 years old. And, well, let's just say that if it wasn't for him I probably wouldn't be here."

"Look," John said. "Charles isn't the same man he used to be. God has really moved in his life and changed him. Man, you don't even know half the stuff Charles used to do. Only God could have pulled him out. Why don't we go back to Charles' house and talk some more."

"Okay." Jacob agreed. "Thanks sis."

"For what?" She asked.

"Just for being you." Charles, John and Jacob left. Harmony closed the door behind them, shook her head and said, "Boys will be boys."

Chapter Ten

TIME BRINGS CHANGE

IT WAS NOW the hottest month of the year. Everyone was complaining about the heat. Harmony's air conditioner was broken, and they were forced to use box fans and ceiling fans for relief. Rick's apartment didn't have central air so he was trying to find a cool place to lie down for the rest of the day. Asia's father invited Harmony, Asia, and Rick over to swim, but Rick didn't go because he said he didn't want to get any darker than he already was. Harmony didn't want to wash her hair later and Asia just didn't want to be around her father and the new friend-wife. Asia made up an excuse about going somewhere with Harmony, but he knew the real reason. After talking to her father, Asia called Harmony.

"Girl, when are you going to let go of what *didn't* happen for your parents?" Harmony asked.

"I don't know how. It's too hard. My mother still loves that man like she did when they first got married and all he does is ignore it. I mean, shouldn't your hearts reciprocate one another's love?"

"I guess it should Asia, but things change and people change. Maybe your father just stopped caring. Eventually you're going to have to face your future step-mother."

"Ew! Why you gotta call her that?"

"Cause, that's what she is. And you're too old to be acting this way. How about you call your Dad back, and agree to meet him at a restaurant. It's public and neutral territory. That way, things can't get ugly."

"Okay, but as long as you and Rick come with me.

"Well, you know you're gonna have to bribe Rick with paying for his meal."

"That's fine. It'll be worth it to have the back up."

Asia called her father and he agreed to meet her, Rick and Harmony at Ma Belle's for dinner.

Harmony was at home cleaning out her closet when the phone rang. It was John and he said he was coming over because he had some news to share with her. About 45 minutes later the doorbell rang and Harmony answered the door. When John saw her face, he smiled immediately. They said hello and shook hands. Then, Harmony invited John in.

"What's up?" she asked. "What's so important?"

"Well, sit down."

Harmony took a seat reluctantly. John grabbed her hands.

"I start seminary in two weeks."

"What? I thought that wouldn't happen for a while."

"That's what I thought as well, but the opportunity has presented itself and I want to take it."

"What did Mr. Langston say?"

"He understood and he's giving me time off to do what God has called me to do."

"He said that?" Harmony asked.

"Yeah. Would you believe that Mr. Langston's father was a circuit preacher and Mr. Langston was called to the ministry as well, but didn't accept the call?"

"Really? Wow! I wonder what that's like."

"I don't know, but it seems like he should be tired of running by now. Well, God has shown us favor and I'm not going to waste it."

"I agree." Harmony added. "But I have some news too. I got the new job and I start in two weeks."

"What? Well, congratulations." John said with hesitance.

"Thanks," she said. "It seems that I came highly recommended by my former boss."

"Yeah, well, I was a bit biased."

"That's okay. I understand how you just can't stop loving me."

"Harmony, I'm concerned about our finances."

"Why? I'll be able to make enough to support us while you're away. And now you can be a kept man for a while." They both laughed.

"Well," John said. "I was thinking that since I'm going to be gone for a long time with seminary, *and* you're going to be starting the new job that maybe we should move the wedding date up."

"Up? Up to where?" Harmony asked.

"Two weeks from now." Just as he said it, he covered his face.

"What?! John no! You just want to stop shaking my hand when we see each other."

"Yes, you're right, but I'll be gone a long time and often. I need something to keep me focused. And, what better way to do that, than to keep my mind on my wife?"

"My love will still be here when you return. And, as far as your mind is concerned, you'd better keep it stayed on Jesus. February 21st is the date and that's final!"

With a groan, John said, "Okay. I've got to go now."

"Where are you going? Are you mad at me?" Harmony asked.

"No." John said. "I have to go tell my parents. I'll call you later."

As he walked away John looked back at Harmony standing in the doorway and she winked at him. He got into the car, and before he closed the door John looked up to the sky and said, "Six months, Lord. Six months!" She closed the front door and John drove off.

With all of the changes taking place in John and Harmony's lives, they had not had much time to choose a place to live. Harmony called Callie and asked her if she'd like to take a drive with her to scout out some apartments. Callie said, "Yes." And, they could catch up on all the events of their lives.

"How's the new job?" Harmony asked.

"How did you know?"

"Mr. Langston called me just before he called you to let me know who he'd chosen.

"Thanks, boss lady. I mean Harmony. Mr. Langston said you really spoke up for me in the interview."

"Callie, you've come a long way in such a short time. Plus, it wasn't just you I was thinking of. It was your babies, too. They can have the Christmas you've wanted to give them with the extra money. Don't you agree?"

"Yeah, I do. So, how are the weddings' plans coming along?"

"They're coming. John starts seminary in two weeks and I start my new job in two weeks. So much is going on right now. I haven't had time to breathe."

"I hear ya, girl. Charles and I have committed to supervised visitation with the kids. And I am going back to school to get my Master in Business."

"Wow! That's great Callie! I'm so proud of you."

"Okay, stop with the business. How was it meeting with the soon-to-be in-laws?"

"Girl, they grilled me up and down. But, I answered all of their questions. John's mother does not like me. Mr. Sutton is okay. Grandfather and Grandmother Sutton are cool, but sometimes his Grandmother confuses me. She's my friend one day and then trying to boss me around the next."

"Maybe she's trying to play both sides of the fence for John's mother's sake.

"Well, she needs to choose 'cause it's making me nervous."

They both laughed and decided to get out and look around the neighborhood.

Pointing to the townhomes on the right Callie says, "These are really beautiful Harmony. Wouldn't you want something a little more, um, "gated"? You know, so the in-laws can't just visit you when they want to."

"Yeah, I guess you're right. Plus, with John becoming a minister, we will need more privacy. Let's look somewhere else," Harmony said.

After a long afternoon of apartment hunting, they decided to get a bite to eat and then call it a day. During their late lunch, early dinner, Callie asked Harmony about infidelity.

"What makes you ask me about that Callie?"

"Harmony, my life has been a rollercoaster for a long time. I've met someone and he is exciting, educated, handsome and wise. He makes me feel like a woman, you know?"

"Is he married?" Harmony asked.

"Why do you ask that?" Callie responded.

"Well, *you're* the one who asked about infidelity."

"Well, yes and no," Callie said.

"Huh?"

"Yes, he's married, but not happily. He's already filed for divorce."

"He told you that?" Harmony asked.

"Yes. Why?"

"It sounds like he's trying to get the milk for free without buying the cow."

"Aw, come on. It's really a fulfilling relationship."

"Does his wife agree?"

"I don't know. I haven't asked her."

"Well ask her and see if she does. If she agrees, then you can move forward with this "relationship." I'm not going to preach to you because you already know what the Word says. But, I want you to really think about what you're doing. There are major consequences to you seeing this man; consequences in life and with God. I think you need to get out while you can. But, you're a grown woman and you can make your own decisions."

"Hey, I gotta get going," Callie said. "I'm meeting him later."

"Okay. Remember what I said, Callie Johnson. But, if anything goes down, I've always got the Vaseline and shoes in the car."

They hugged one another and Callie left. Harmony's cell phone rang. It was Asia.

"Hey, my father called. We're meeting him this Saturday. Are you still free?"

"Uh, yeah. Have you called Rick yet?"

"He can't make it. He's got appointments, he said."

"Alright! Do you want me to bring John?"

"Yeah, that would be great. My father won't cuss in front of a minister."

"Cool, see you Saturday."

The atmosphere with Asia's father was stiff. Harmony wasn't sure if she should sit between Asia and her father, or between Asia and the new lady. She decided to sit next to John.

"Where's the new girlfriend?" Asia asked.

"Uh, do you mean soon-to-be wife?" Asia's father responded.

"Dad! You're still married to mom. You've already proposed to her?" Callie exclaimed.

"No. Not yet, but I plan to very soon. She's running a little late. Asia, she's a great girl. She's educated and nice to look at. She knows me like no other woman could. She makes me feel young again, and she loves my singing in the shower."

"Ugh, do you have to give the details?"

Asia looked over at John and Harmony for help, but none came. After a long silence, Mr. Hart excused himself and went to the men's room. Asia left to take in some fresh air. Just then, Callie came over to the table and saw John and Harmony.

"Hey girl. What are you two doing here?"

"We're having dinner with my best friend, Asia and her father. What about you?"

"I'm here to have dinner with William and his daughter."

"Oh My Lord! Callie, is the man you're seeing William Hart?"

"Yeah, how'd you know?"

"Because that's my best friend's father's name. Girl, you have got to get out of here."

"Do we need to have a quick prayer?" John asked.

"You'd better make it a long one. I've gotta stall Asia outside before she comes back in."

Just as Harmony was leaving to find Asia, Mr. Hart returned to the table and started speaking to John about the upcoming nuptials.

"Are you ready?" Mr. Hart asked.

"Yes. Are you?" John asked.

"Excuse me?" Mr. Hart replied.

As John looked up and saw Asia coming back to the table without Harmony, and with Callie sitting at the table, John said, "Let's have a word of prayer."

"Huh?" Mr. Hart said.

John began to pray.

"Hello. I'm Asia. And, you are?"

"Callie. Nice to meet you."

"Asia, it seems that Callie and Harmony know each other." Mr. Hart stated.

"Really? How?"

"We work together. Or we used to, and I'm in the wedding party." Callie claimed.

"Really? Harmony never mentioned you. What part do you play in her wedding?"

"I was hoping to be the maid of honor, but she told me that position was filled a long time ago."

"Oh, I see," Asia said.

"Amen!" John said.

They looked over at him to see what he was babbling about. Harmony returned to the table and wondered if she had walked into the eye of the storm. The waiter came over to their table to take their orders. After the waiter left, John opened up another conversation concerning the weather. Harmony tried to keep it going, but the overcast skies outside had nothing to do with what was going on at this moment at their table.

Everyone was silent during dinner. Asia was disgusted at the fact that her father would hook up with a woman so young. And, that her mother was at home nursing a wound that she felt would never heal. Callie was all over Mr. Hart as if he were going to be snatched up at any moment. John just kept his head down while he finished his meal. Asia broke the silence.

"Dad, I have to go. I can't condone this relationship."

"Honey, sit down please!"

"No, Dad. I can't pretend that I am happy for you. I'm really hurting right now and I need to leave before I say something that isn't pleasing in God's sight."

"We'll go with you, Asia." Harmony said.

John and Harmony excused themselves. As they were preparing to leave, John went back to the table and said, "God bless you." They left Callie and Mr. Hart alone at the table. Just then, the waiter came over.

"Sir, would you like dessert?" The waiter asked.

"No thank you. We're done," Mr. Hart said in a sad tone.

Chapter Eleven

'TIS THE SEASON TO WHAT?

Mrs. Wilkes had now been cancer-free for over a year. Harmony's parents were closer than ever. Mr. Wilkes hadn't been feeling very well for a while now, but Harmony assumed that it was because she was getting married soon. It was probably something that most fathers go through right before they give their little girl away. Asia and her father were barely speaking to one another. Though each of them missed the other, both were too stubborn to budge. Callie was still seeing Mr. Hart, but not as much. It was hard for her to break away from the man she loved. She and Harmony didn't discuss the relationship too often. Harmony poured herself into her new job and wedding planning. Things were coming together on time. She missed John.

The holidays were fast-approaching. Everyone decided to spend Thanksgiving with their own families. John was home for the weekend and Harmony wanted him to spend his last Thanksgiving as a single man with his parents and grandparents. John and Harmony had just over two months before the big day.

"Are you ready, Princess?" Mr. Wilkes asked.

"Yes, Daddy. I'm ready. Are you feeling okay?" she asked him.

"Just tired, I guess. Your mother has me going from store to store to find her ingredients."

"Well, you know how Ma likes to have her pots in order. It'll be great, you'll see."

"It always is." Mr. Wilkes added.

Just as Mr. Wilkes predicted, the food was delicious. Harmony and Jacob washed the dishes and decided to go out afterwards to walk off the food. While they were out, Harmony asked Jacob if he noticed their father's behavior.

"He's probably nervous about the wedding. You know how Dad feels about you."

"Yeah, I guess. But it seems like it's more than that. I hope you're right, Jake. So how's your love life? And, how is the new job at United Aerospace, Inc?"

"It's great! I really want to thank John for putting in a good word for me with Mr. Langston."

"John's crazy about you, Jacob. You're the brother he never had."

"Say, Harmony, how do you feel about Shondra?"

"Oh wow, Shondra. I haven't spoken to her in a while, why?"

"We seem to get along pretty well and I was thinking of asking her out."

"Well, when I worked with her, she was a big gossip. We didn't get along very well. But as a worker, she's cool. Just be careful. As Ma' would tell you, pray about any and every situation."

"Always the preacher's wife huh?" Jacob said.

"Yeah. I guess I will be pretty soon."

"How do you feel about that, Harmony?"

"It's exciting and a little scary. It's not that I'm afraid of what God will do with us as a couple; I'm afraid I won't stand up to what people expect of me, especially John's mother."

"Harmony, no mother wants her "baby boy" to grow up, least of all, get married. Just stick to your guns. Trust God and nobody else. What does John say?"

"Jon says the same thing. I guess that's why you two get along so well. What's it like to have sex, Jacob?"

"Whoa! That's personal."

"I don't want the details; I can use my own imagination."

"What's it like to join with a woman in that way? What did you feel? I mean, besides the obvious."

"Well, it wasn't what I thought it would be. Even though it wasn't a one-time thing, it was never mind blowing. It just was. You know how they say it is in the movies, well, that doesn't happen. At least, it didn't for me. I'm glad you waited for the right man to come along. You two can learn from each other and keep God in it. That way, I think it will be beautiful."

"Hey, you want to sleep in front of the mall tonight so we can catch the big sales tomorrow? Just for old times' sake?" Harmony asked.

"Okay." Jacob said. "Is it just you and me?"

"Sure. That's fine. We can do like we used to and bring the popcorn, drinks and music. I miss hanging out with my big brother."

"Likewise, little sis. Likewise."

As they approached the house, Harmony saw John's car parked out front. She ran inside and ran straight to him.

"What are you doing here? Is anything wrong?" Harmony asked.

"No, just wanted to see you. Can we talk outside?"

"Sure. What's up?"

"My parents, well, my mother wants to have Christmas dinner at her house. She wants to combine Christmas dinner with our wedding party so that she can add some more details."

"What kind of details?"

"I'm not sure, but I heard her talking to my grandmother about singing."

"What? Your mother can't sing, can she?"

"She can hold a note in a cup and that's all."

"John what are we going to tell her?"

"I left immediately after I heard her talking."

"Well, let me talk to my mom and dad about this. My family has a long honored tradition of celebrating Christmas in the weirdest way. We cook, eat, then cook and eat some more. Then after we've eaten ourselves silly, we go back to bed then open our gifts really late at night."

"That's different." John said.

"Yeah, and my Uncle Lionel comes over at that time. We only see him once or twice a year, if that. But we do get cards in the mail from his many trips all over the country."

"Okay. I just thought I'd let you know so that you can be ready."

John left and Jacob and Harmony went upstairs to get their survival kits for spending the night on the street. Mr. Wilkes knocked on Harmony's bedroom door.

"Come in!"

"Where are you going, Princess?"

"Jacob and I are going to spend the night at the mall so that we can catch the sales."

"You two haven't done that in a while. Hey, I want to tell you something."

"Yes, Daddy?"

"I'm so proud of you and your decision to wait on God. You've made your mother and me very happy with your career decisions, your Christian walk and your choice of a husband. Remember Princess, John isn't perfect and he never will be. Being a minister is a big responsibility and John's going to need a strong support system while he's away and when he's at home. There will be many women with so called "issues" to talk to him about. But don't you get jealous or envious. Don't press him about how much time he's spending doing "God's work.""

"Oh Daddy. I won't do that."

"Harmony, you know how you can be. Love and commitment need to be the band-aid that covers all the wounds. God will do the healing underneath. I want plenty of grandbabies, too. But I think you and John need to wait to have a family until his schedule gets a little more stable. Raising kids is hard, too. Your mother and I had to struggle, but we made it. When I was a musician, I had a lot of groupies. I made the mistake of kissing one of them while

I was married to your mother. Your mother being pregnant with you was great and all, but we didn't have a lot of money. I wasn't communicating very well with your mom. There was a woman who gave me the attention I needed and wanted.

One night your mom surprised me and showed up at the club. I wasn't having a good night. My lead singer didn't show up. The drummer was nursing his wounds from a broken relationship so he was always off beat. During one of my breaks, I went into the back room and there was a woman at the office door. She said she was there to comfort me. Your mom saw everything. It was only a kiss, well, several kisses, but it wasn't right. I hurt your mother dearly. It took us a while to get back what we had, but we did and when you were born, I made a vow to God that I wouldn't make that mistake again. And I haven't."

"Daddy, why did you do it?"

"I felt like a failure Princess. I was a musician with a son and a baby on the way. I was in school and I couldn't take the pressure. I left that gig and went to another club for less pay. Even though I didn't make the money I was making at the other place, it was worth it for my family. I don't regret it one bit. I love you, Princess."

"Why are you telling me all this now?"

"Well, it was on my mind and I figured I'd tell you now."

"Thanks for telling me Daddy."

"Are you mad at me?"

"No. A little disappointed. I never thought you would have done something like that. Ma never told me."

"She promised she wouldn't."

"Does Jake know?"

"Yes. I told him after he got into that mix up with Callie. You guys be careful and have fun. Don't spend all of your money in one place."

"Yes Sir."

"Good night, Princess."

"Good night, Daddy. I Love you."

Jacob and Harmony were all set to wait all night to catch the sales. It was freezing downtown. The hot chocolate had gotten cold and the sun wasn't coming up fast enough. They decided to go home, get some sleep and then catch the sales later the next day.

Morning came and Harmony went in to wake up Jacob, but he wasn't getting up so she decided to go alone. She was looking for Christmas presents for her family, for John, and her wedding party. She decided to get John a sterling silver keychain with a heart carved into it. She had her name engraved on it, and had them gift wrap it for her. She got her mom a silk blue scarf; and for Jacob, a gift card to his favorite sports store. She bought Asia and Rick driving gloves. For the girls in her wedding party, she bought gift baskets full of soaps, bubble bath and towels. And, for her father, she bought an autographed saxophone CD by his favorite artist. Along with the CD, she purchased tickets to a night of Jazz for her Mom and Dad as a thank you.

When Harmony arrived home she took her bags to her room and hid them under her bed. Everyone was awake and watching television. She decided to use this time to speak to her family about what John's mother had suggested for the wedding party. Mrs. Wilkes was all for it. Mr. Wilkes wanted to know if he had to dress all fancy in order to attend.

"Dad, you can wear what you want. It's not about that."

"Alright. We can go." Everyone agreed.

Mrs. Wilkes offered to bring her famous sweet potato pie and macaroni and cheese.

Thanksgiving weekend was now over, and it was back to work for Harmony. John had to head back to Seminary. Harmony and John said their good-bye's with hesitation. Harmony was just as busy at the new job as she had been at Langston Aerospace. She was so tired at the end of the day that when she arrived home she went to bed immediately; many times without dinner.

John called, but she didn't pick up her cell phone. When she woke up and realized she had missed his call, she was sad. She had promised that she would make time for him. She called him back, but there was no answer. There was a voicemail from him. She listened to it over and over because she missed his voice.

"Hi Harm. It's me. I wanted to hear your voice. I guess you're busy. I will try to reach you later. I love you."

She went downstairs to see what everyone was doing. Mrs. Wilkes was writing down what she needed in order to cook her famous pies and macaroni and cheese. Jacob had gone out with some friends, and Mr. Wilkes was in the living room watching television. Rather, it was watching him. He had fallen asleep in front of the TV again.

"Ma, do you need any help with anything?" Harmony asked"

"No baby, I'm good. Did you get a good nap?"

"Yes. But I missed John's call."

"Well, I'm sure he'll understand."

Just then the house phone rang and Harmony answered. It was Uncle Lionel. He asked all of the usual questions, "when's dinner, where's dinner and what y'all doin'?" Harmony put him on the speaker phone so her mom could hear him also.

"Hey, we miss you." Mrs. Wilkes said.

"Where's dinner?" Uncle Lionel asked.

"Dinner is at the Sutton's home this year." Mrs. Wilkes answered.

"Yeah, John's mother invited all of us over. We're not doing much. Where are you this week?" Harmony asked.

"I'm home. I just got back from Florida. The weather was beautiful!"

"Did you meet someone?" asked Mrs. Wilkes.

"No meddling Belle."

"I'm sorry. I just want you to be happy."

"I'm fine, Belle. How's the family? Are the wedding plans coming along okay? Am I still invited?"

"Of course you're invited, Uncle Lionel. You'll be sitting with Ma and Dad."

"Belle, how did Joe's doctor's appointment go?"

As quick as she could, Mrs. Wilkes turned off the speaker phone and picked up the receiver. With a shaky voice she said, "He's fine, Lionel. Just gas is all."

"Oh, okay. Well, I have to get going. I'll see you at Christmas dinner."

"Okay, stay safe and I love you."

"Love you too, Sis."

Mrs. Wilkes hung up the phone and hoped that Harmony wasn't going to question what she had heard.

"Ma. What's wrong with Dad?"

"Just a check-up is all. He hasn't been feeling too well these past few of months. I thought it would pass, but it hasn't. Doctor says its severe gas."

"Does he need to stop eating certain foods?"

"Probably, but you know your father. He loves his soul food. We just have to keep praying for him. Are you and Jacob going to set up the Christmas tree this weekend?" Changing the subject.

"I'm not sure. Jacob's been M.I.A. lately. It's probably a girl."

"Well, I hope it's not who he asked me about on Thanksgiving."

"Who?" Mrs. Wilkes asked.

"Just a girl I used to work with. I told Jacob she used to be a big gossip. I pray he makes the right decision."

"Harmony, can you do me a favor?"

"Yes, Ma. What is it?"

"Stay close to your brother for your father's sake. You two need to stay close and keep the ties strong."

"Uh, okay."

Harmony wondered what that meant. She decided to call Asia and Rick. They were on three-way and she told them all of what her father had said to her on Thanksgiving and what her mother had just told her.

"I think something is up you guys."

"Me too." Asia said. "But why wouldn't they tell you if it were?"

"Maybe they don't want you to worry." Rick said. "Especially with your wedding day so close and all."

"I pray it's nothing serious." Harmony said.

"Us too." Rick and Asia both said.

"So, is there a dress code for Christmas dinner?" Rick asked.

"No. Casual dress is fine." Harmony responded.

"Are we going to have to put our napkins on our laps?" Asia asked.

"No, but please don't have your cell phones on while you're at the table. Mrs. Sutton and Grandma Maddie hate that!"

The next few weeks went by quickly. John and Harmony couldn't wait until Christmas Day when they'd be able to see each other again. They were excited to exchange gifts for the last time as single people.

Mrs. Sutton decided to segregate the families. The Wilkes and guests sat on one side, and the Suttons and guests on the other. Grandma Maddie and Grandpa Rufus were sitting at the far end of the table. Pastor Sutton sat at the head of the table and Mrs. Sutton sat to his right. The blessing of the food was given by John. Not much conversation was done at the table because the Suttons didn't do that sort of thing. The food was tasty. The traditional Christmas dinner was not served. They ate chicken curry with Masala herbs, small salad, rice pilaf, and dinner rolls. Even though the macaroni and cheese didn't go with the chicken curry they added it to the table's menu. They gobbled up Mrs. Wilkes' pies. No one touched Mrs. Sutton's pies. As a beverage Grandma Maddie made sweet tea. She said the liquor bottles were empty. Mrs. Sutton decided to ask Harmony about how they'd survive without John's income.

"Well, I'm prepared to allow John to do what God has called him to do. The Lord will work it out for us."

Meredith pursed her lips and sat down.

"Meredith, do you need something to drink?" Pastor Sutton asked.

"No. I'm fine dear."

He then grabbed her by her arm and pulled her into the kitchen.

"What are you doing, Meredith!?"

"Nothing, just making sure she's going to take care of my baby."

111

"He's a grown man, Meredith, and he'll be fine. If you can't behave yourself, you will go to your room. Is that understood?" Pastor Sutton said.

"Yes," she said reluctantly.

Grandma Maddie asked Harmony if she could make her wedding handkerchief. Harmony was touched by the gesture.

"Thank you. That would be lovely." Harmony said.

"How many girls will you have on your side?" Nettie asked.

"I have you as my junior bride. Asia is my maid of honor. Callie will be my bridesmaid. So, I guess that's three."

"No flower girl?" Nettie asked.

"No. We're doing something different. We won't show you until the day of the wedding."

"How can you hide things from us Harmony? We're in the wedding too!" Mrs. Sutton said.

"Meredith!?" Mr. Sutton called out. "That's two!"

"What kind of dresses are you wearing?" Grandma Maddie asked.

"The dresses are baby blue. They are draped in the front and back. The dresses are satin and each lady will carry white roses."

"They sound like stripper dresses to me." Mrs. Sutton said. "Will they be carrying a pole along with the roses?"

"Meredith Baxter Sutton! Go to your room now! I'm sorry, everyone," Mr. Sutton said.

"No problem, Mr. Sutton." Asia said. That's not a bad idea. That way, at the reception, we can really have some fun because John and Harmony don't dance."

Callie gave Asia a high-five. That was the first time they had agreed on anything.

Mrs. Wilkes told Grandma Maddie that she understood how Meredith felt about losing her son, but that this was ordained in Heaven a long time ago and there was nothing she could do about it.

"Amen!" said Grandpa Rufus.

The others began side conversations about various things. While that was going on Charles went over to talk to Callie during all of the discussions. Charles asked Callie if they could speak privately outside.

Holding her hand and staring into her eyes he said, "I miss you Callie." I want you back."

"Charles what are you talking about?"

"God has truly shown me where I need to be. And it's with you and the kids. I know you're probably seeing someone, but he can't love you like I can. And our family will be blessed. I'll never stop loving you or fighting for you."

Callie was speechless and felt a bit perplexed by it all. She turned away from him and shook her head. Charles walked back inside and went over to John to talk. Callie followed after and sat in the living room. Jacob went outside to get some air and called Shondra.

"Can you meet me at my house in an hour?" Jacob asked.

"Sure." Shondra replied.

"Thanks."

Jacob went back inside and stayed for another twenty minutes and then excused himself. That was the cue for everyone to leave. Since Meredith had been banned to her room, the rest of the planning continued without interruption.

"We'll talk to you all later," Mr. Wilkes said.

John and Harmony decided to stick around a little longer.

On the way home, Mrs. Wilkes complained about John's mother's behavior. "Belle, I don't feel too good right now. Can we talk about this later?"

"Sure." She said.

She looked over at her husband holding his stomach and began to pray.

"We're almost home, Joe. Hold on."

John and Harmony went outside to exchange gifts. They got each other the same thing. All they could do was smile at each other.

"Now you really have the key to my heart." Harmony said.

"As do you for me." said John.

This time, they hugged and held on to one another.

Chapter Twelve

HAPPY NEW YEAR?

T HE HOLIDAYS WENT by quickly. Mr. Wilkes cried when he opened up the Christmas gift Harmony gave to him. Mrs. Wilkes screamed with excitement when she saw the beautiful scarf. Jacob just said thanks and went upstairs to talk to Shondra on the phone. Asia and Rick wore their gloves proudly. The bridesmaids had to wait until the day before the wedding to receive their gifts.

Asia and Callie were getting along better now. Whatever Charles said to Callie at the Christmas dinner really made her think about her life and the changes she needed to make. Jacob and Shondra were dating regularly, but Jacob said he wouldn't get serious too soon like he had with LaTonya. He wanted to take things slow. Shondra didn't attend church like Jacob, but he didn't mind. He figured he could change her mind after a lot of dating and spending time together. Harmony, the skeptic, didn't trust her.

Mr. and Mrs. Wilkes were a lot quieter these days. They spent a lot of time in their room talking. Harmony and Jacob figured that the holiday season had worn both of them out. Harmony found her rhythm in her new position. Since she came from a very prestigious company, no one was offering much help to her. She had to learn by trial and error, and at first it seemed like more error.

John was out of town and Harmony found herself doing the final running around for the wedding, alone. She wasn't bothered by it because doing so gave her a chance to think about what was getting ready to take place in her personal life. At the same time she wanted him with her.

"A preacher's wife? Wow!" I am going to be a preacher's wife," she said out loud.

It sounded different coming from her lips than when someone else said it. She thought back on what she had been through, and how God had seen her through so many things in her life; the tragedy with Tony in high school; graduating from college, twice; a family who loves her; and, two of the very best friends in the world who always had her back. And now, they were all successful in their careers. Her mother's cancer was in remission and John was so in-love with her that he couldn't help but smile when she was around him. All she could say was, "Thank you, Lord." Harmony decided to call Nettie and see if she wanted to hang out for a while.

"Yes!" Nettie said.

They went to a "hole-in-wall" burger place. The food was so messy and so good. They both licked their hands instead of using napkins.

"How's school?" Harmony asked Nettie.

"It's school. I don't think any of the boys there like me."

"Why do you say that?"

"Because they're always hitting me and calling me names."

"That means they *do* like you." Harmony laughed.

"Really?"

"Boys don't know how to express themselves like we do, especially at that age. They act like cave men and they think girls are supposed to know what it means."

"Oh." Nettie said. "Harmony, I have a question. What's a period?"

Harmony choked a little while drinking her soda.

"Huh? Have you asked your mother about that?"

"Yes, but she's so caught up with John leaving that it's the only thing she talks about."

"How about we finish our food first, then we can take a drive and have a little girl talk."

"Okay," Nettie said.

While Nettie was finishing her food, Harmony was sending up a silent prayer asking God for guidance.

"I'm ready!" Nettie said.

"Okay, let's go."

During the drive there were times when Nettie would get grossed out and didn't want to hear anymore. But she kept asking questions.

"How long should I wait to have sex?" Nettie asked.

"Until you're married!" Harmony demanded.

"Why? My mom didn't wait."

"How do you know that?"

"Because I overheard my grandparents and my mom talking about it one night and my mom was saying that you probably aren't a virgin, and that you are pretending to be one. So my grandfather said, "Oh, like *you* were, Meredith when you got married?"

Harmony laughed out loud.

"You are my favorite little sister Nettie. Thanks for the info. You really should wait until you're married. In 1 Corinthians 6:15-20, it talks about how our bodies are members of Christ. Anyone who joins himself (meaning has sex) is one body with her. And the two shall become one. You are to flee sexual immorality. Every other sin that a man commits is outside the body, but the sexually immoral person sins against his own body, and your body is a temple of the Holy Spirit within you, whom you have from God. You're not your own Nettie, and you were bought with a price. So glorify God in your body."

Harmony left out the part where it says prostitute because she didn't think Nettie would understand that word.

"What does that mean?" Nettie asked.

"It means that when you decide to have sex with someone, because God designed sex for marriage, you automatically become one with that person. And like it says, your body is not yours; it belongs to God. You have been bought with a price; a very valuable price."

Nettie was looking confused.

"Okay, suppose you were buying candy at the store. But, the candy didn't come in wrappers. It was only available as open candy in a jar. Everyone that wanted that candy stuck their hands in the jar and got a piece. Now, who knows if the people before you wiped their nose, or even licked their fingers, or they didn't wash their hands before they put their hand in the jar? That candy should have a wrapper on it because it was set aside for only one person to buy. If everyone puts their hand in the candy jar would you really want to eat some of it?"

"No, 'cause it would be nasty." Nettie said.

"Exactly! In the same way, God has picked out one person in your life to have *your* candy. And, if you allow someone to open your wrapper and take a bite of your candy, then, when the man who is supposed to have your candy gets there, he may not want it because it's been touched already. Your candy will have become one with too many hands. Does that make sense?"

"Yes, sort of."

"So, what are you going to do now?" Harmony asked.

"I'm going to keep my candy *all* to myself. I'm not sharing with anyone except my husband. And, Harmony, it's going to be *so* sweet because I waited on God and for him to un-wrap me."

"You've got it, little sis."

Harmony dropped Nettie back off at home and before she got out of the car, Nettie gave her a big hug.

"Thank you for today. I had fun." Nettie said.

"You're welcome."

Harmony reached over and gave Nettie a candy bar. They both laughed and Nettie said she was going to keep it until the right buyer came. On the drive home, Harmony felt good about her conversation with Nettie. She was starting to feel like a big sister now. Harmony's cell phone rang. It was John.

"Hi there!" she said. "How are you?"

I'm missing you very much, Michelle. I can't wait to see you."

"I can't wait to see you either, John. How are your studies going?"

"They're going. I'm a little tired, but God is definitely allowing me to complete my assignments on time. I know that I won't make it up here without Him."

"I just spent the afternoon with Nettie."

"How was that?"

"Fun and interesting. Your sister is a good girl."

"Well, what did you guys do?"

"We just ate and talked about girl stuff."

"What? Harmony, I don't think it's your place to say anything to her about that."

"What do you mean? She had questions and besides that, we're about to be family."

"You should leave that kind of stuff to my mother."

"Your mother is too busy putting me down and stressing over you marrying me to spend any time with Nettie."

"Well, what did you tell her?"

"I told her the truth, John. What's the big deal? If I hadn't answered her questions, she might have gone to someone that would steer her wrong. Or, worse, some raggedy little boy who would try to show her what to do."

"Does my mother know?"

"I don't know. It's up to Nettie if she wants to tell her."

"Well, I'm going to tell her so that Nettie doesn't get in trouble."

"John, it's not that serious. Why are you making such a big deal out of this?"

"Look, let me worry about that. I just wanted to say "hi". I'll call you again later."

He hung up the phone and Harmony began to cry.

"Oh Lord," she said aloud. "Is this how it's going to be from now on?"

The next morning, John called.

"Hey, Harm. I'm sorry for what I said. Sometimes, I can be just like my mother with things. The Lord really convicted me last night. I'm glad that Nettie had you to talk to. Can you forgive me?"

"I already have." Harmony said.

"We've only got three weeks, Michelle, until we can stop shaking hands."

"Yeah, I know," she said in a sensual tone.

"What's wrong, Harm?"

"John, is your mother going to be a major issue when we get married? I don't want her making decisions through you for our lives. We're depending on God and God alone, right?"

"Yes, of course. I'm sorry. It's just that she has had a big influence on me and my decisions. She's very old-fashioned."

"Not in the sex department." Harmony said under her breath.

"What did you say?"

"Nothing."

"Okay."

"Don't forget when you get home, we have a counseling session the next evening."

"Oh, okay. Rev. Pyle, right?"

"Yes. Remember we had to find someone neutral who wouldn't be biased.

"Okay. I've got to go to class. I'll talk to you soon. I love you, Michelle."

"I love you too, John."

A week later, John came home and he was looking *good* to his fiancé right about now. She missed him a great deal. She wore his favorite color - blue. He wore a dark blue polo shirt and some slacks. "Such a minister," she thought. But, that's her man. The counseling session lasted about two hours. During the session Reverend Pyle asked Harmony if she was ready to take on all the responsibilities and demands of a minister's wife.

"Yes. I am." She replied with certainty.

"It's not easy living under a microscope Harmony. All you do publicly and privately will be scrutinized."

"She's ready Pastor Lyle. I believe in her and us." John said.

"Okay John. I'm not the enemy. I support this union. I remember what it was like for me and my wife in the beginning. Harmony, maybe you can speak to John's mother about her initial experiences."

"No!" they both said in agreement.

"I understand. Let me pray for you so you can get home."

Afterwards, John and Harmony went to dinner.

"Are you ready Harmony?" John asked.

"Ready for what?" she replied.

"To be my wife." John stated.

"Not you too John. Of course I am. I will admit that being a preacher's wife will be a challenge, but we've got a good support system in place. I believe in my heart we'll be fine.

Harmony paused for a moment as if to allow what she said sink in.

"What other dreams do you have John?"

"What do you mean?"

"I mean, coupled with ministry, what dreams do you have for the church and for us?"

"As far as the church goes, I want what God wants. Being the youth minister in a church that size will be something to see God work through, but I've been talking to my father and we've agreed that we need to do something concerning our youth and our senior citizens. They need something of their own to nurture, love and watch grow. There is a great need in the Youth Department for leadership, but no one will step up. I have definitely been praying in that area that God will use not only me, but us as a couple. You are very good with children and teenagers. I think you should look into the possibility of working with them."

"I'll pray on it." Harmony answered.

"Concerning us, I have a dream that we'll have at least eight kids, seven boys and one girl."

"Why only one girl?"

"Because I don't think I could handle more than one. And this way, her brothers could always look out for her. She'll have a lot of back up."

"Why eight kids?"

"I don't know. Maybe it's because I come from a small family."

"I do love children. We'll pray on that one too. Big time!"

"I'd like us to be a couple that God uses tremendously. I am more than excited to be your husband Harmony, and I promise to do my best to love you with God's love." Harmony looked at him differently this time. She had an assurance of this man and his calling to be her husband, best friend, and some day her Pastor.

They finished dinner and drove down to the square for a walk. Now that they were almost married, Harmony and John held hands. She was still sticking to her guns about not kissing him until they were married. John didn't mind. He said she was worth the wait.

"I don't want you to leave again." Harmony said.

"I don't want to go either. But you know I have to."

"What time does your plane leave?"

"Noon. Why?"

"I'll be at work."

"Don't worry. My father is dropping me off at the airport."

"I wish I didn't have to present a proposal tomorrow."

"You have to work. You're supporting me, remember?"

Harmony tried to give John a mean look and they both laughed. John drove Harmony home and walked her inside. Mrs. Wilkes walked in from the kitchen.

"Hi Son. How are you?"

"I'm fine, Mrs. Wilkes."

He walked over and gave her a hug.

"How's Mr. Wilkes doing?"

"He's fine. He just went to bed early."

"He's been doing that a lot lately, Ma." Harmony said.

"Child, your father isn't as young as he used to be. Neither one of us is, but he's fine. Good to see you again, John. Take care."

Mrs. Wilkes went upstairs to give them some privacy.

"What's wrong Harmony?"

"My father has been acting funny lately and sleeping a lot. I think something is wrong."

"You heard your mother; maybe he's just getting older. Hey look, I've got to run. My dad and I are going to have a man-to-man talk tonight."

"Good luck with that."

She walked him to the door, gave him a hug, shook his hand and said good-night. Harmony watched John drive away then walked into the kitchen to get some juice from the fridge when her cell phone rang.

"Hey Sis!" Jacob said.

"Hey, what's up?"

"Nothing much. I need a favor."

"What?"

"I need you to come down and bail me out of jail."

"What!? Jacob, what happened?"

"I'll explain when you get here, and don't say nothin' to Ma and Dad."

"Okay, I won't."

During the drive over, Harmony said a prayer. "This had better be good," she thought. When Harmony arrived at the police station, she talked to the clerk about bailing out her brother. She asked if she could see him first. The clerk took her back to see Jacob, but he wasn't allowed to come to the window. She could only see him from a distance. Harmony bailed him out and they headed for the parking lot. In the car, she asked him what happened.

"Remember Shondra?"

"Yeah. Why?"

"She and I were at The Spot, the club over on Eighth Street. We were dancing and everything was goin' fine. Then this guy walked up and told me to let go of his woman. Shondra said to him, *"I ain't your woman no more."* We went back to dancing, and then, this same dude, who stands at least 6'8, hit me across my face and knocked me clear across the room. I got up to hit him back, but he put his arm on my face to hold me. So I did what you girls do; I kicked him in his groin. The guy was hurting real bad and the security guards came in to break it up. Shondra ran away and the other guy and I got arrested for disturbing the peace."

"Didn't I tell you that I had a bad feeling about that girl? Jacob, how long will you go on like this? You gotta start making better decisions. You're lucky Ma and Dad are asleep."

When they got home, Mrs. Wilkes was coming down the stairs.

"What are you doing up, Ma?!" Jacob asked.

"Gettin' some water. Is that okay?"

"Yeah, I'm sorry. I didn't mean to sound that way."

"Are you okay, Son?"

"Yes, I'm fine. I just got a headache."

"Alright now. Good night you two and don't stay up too late."

"We won't," they said together.

Harmony walked over to Jacob and slapped him upside his head.

"Ow! Why'd you do that?"

"Because you don't listen. Who's the oldest Jacob?

"I am!" He answered.

"Then act like it! Good night!" Harmony whispered.

Harmony left him downstairs to fend for himself. Jacob watched television and decided to call Shondra.

"Hey, that was downright dirty what you did to me back there, girl."

"I'm sorry, Jacob, I couldn't stay."

"Come on baby!" Jacob could hear in the background.

"Who's that?"

"Uh, that's my friend."

"Your friend, who?"

"The guy you were fighting with in the club."

"I'm done with you Shondra. Girl, you a hot mess!" Jacob hung up the phone and went to his room. That night Jacob thought a lot about what Harmony said to him. He needs to make some changes now!

Jacob woke up with a throbbing headache, but he still had to go to work, and he had to face Shondra. Before Jacob could get into the office, Callie walked up to him and asked him how he was feeling.

"You know?"

"Man, everybody knows. Shondra can't keep a secret. Leave her alone Jacob." Callie said. "She's nothing but trouble."

"I hear you," said Jacob. "I'm done with her."

"Did you sleep with her?"

"No. Why?"

"Good, 'cause from what I hear, that girl is mean in the bedroom and you wouldn't be able to recover if you know what I mean. God bless you, my brother. Uh, boss!"

Jacob went into his office and called Callie in.

"What's the morning report, Ms. Johnson?" Callie gave him all of the files to be reviewed and passed along.

"Good work. My sister said that you were good at your job."

"Yes. She's right! Thanks boss."

Callie left his office to get back to work. On the way to her desk, she stopped at Shondra's cubicle.

"Don't screw with him again. If you do, you deal with me, you hear? Have a good day."

Callie sashed down the hall back to her desk.

Shondra just looked at her and swallowed hard. She knew Callie was from the hood, and deep down inside she was serious. Though she had gotten back into church, the old Callie was still alive and well.

Chapter Thirteen

It's Time!

~~~~~~~~~~~~~~~~~~~~~~~~~~~~~~~~~~~~

THE WEDDING DAY is upon them. John is back in town and everything is in order. Mrs. Sutton had calmed down a little. Grandma Maddie had been keeping an eye on her for Pastor Sutton. Grandpa Rufus was working on his reception speech consistently. Nettie couldn't wait to wear her dress and the congregation was ecstatic!

John and Harmony decided there would not be a wedding rehearsal dinner. Everyone just wanted to go home, and John and Harmony had a surprise they needed to work on. Charles and Jacob made sure John had all he needed at the church. Afterwards, Charles and Jacob went over to Charles' apartment to chill. Mr. Wilkes needed to talk privately to Harmony one last time so they went into the sanctuary.

The wedding coordinators had done an excellent job with putting together their winter wonderland design. Harmony and John were specific about everything. Roses filled the sanctuary. Each pew panel had a small bouquet of white roses draped from the top of them with one red rose in the middle to signify John and Harmony's love. They were tied with a dark blue and light blue ribbon. White tulle was draped from the ceiling, corner to corner with white, icicle lights inside to create the stars. Mr. Wilkes and Harmony went over to a pew that wasn't decorated to sit down and talk.

"I just wanted to give you something Princess."

Mr. Wilkes pulled a red, velvet box out of his pocket and handed it to her. When Harmony opened it, there were three single diamonds in it. Harmony was at a loss for words.

"They symbolize something very significant to me. One diamond came from my mother's ring. The second one came from your mother's ring. The third one is to be placed into *your* Mother's ring when you have your first daughter. Diamonds are forever, like my love for you, Princess. I'm so proud of you."

"Thank you Daddy. I'll never forget this day as long as I live."

They both began to cry. So much that they cried into each other's arms. Mr. Wilkes cried more than Harmony. He wasn't ready to let her go so they sat there a little longer.

"Thank you, Daddy. I'll put it in a ring as soon as I have my first daughter. But what if I have all boys?"

"Then still put it in a ring and tell them that whomever gets married first will give that ring to his fiancé, and she'd better be priceless like his mother."

They heard someone clear their throat. It was John. They dried their eyes and Mr. Wilkes stood up and walked her over to John.

"Take good care of her or God won't bless you." Mr. Wilkes said.

"I will Sir," said John. "You can count on it."

Mr. Wilkes walked out of the sanctuary.

"You okay?" John asked.

"Yes. Just father-daughter stuff."

She finished wiping her eyes, and John and Harmony went to work on their surprise. They only had a couple of hours because Callie and Asia were coming to pick her up so that they could get her ready for her big day tomorrow. Jacob and Charles would be there soon also. Harmony and John finished their private project and smiled.

"It's going to be beautiful," they both said aloud.

"No, Michelle. You're going to be beautiful."

They shook hands one last time, and then parted ways.

They both had a hard time sleeping. Harmony opened her blinds to stare at the night sky. She enjoyed looking at the moon and stars at night. Harmony began to feel sleepy so she turned away from the window. Before she closed her eyes she turned back to the window, looked up at the sky and said, "Thank you Lord."

The next morning, Asia, Callie and Rick had a lavish breakfast, make-up and hair presentation set-up for Harmony at Callie's house. She wanted for nothing. Rick will do the hair of the bridesmaids, junior bride, and maid of honor first. Charles and Jacob had a surprise for John as well. Harmony and John didn't want the traditional parties that brides and grooms usually have, so their friends decided to treat them like royalty instead. The ceremony was scheduled to begin at one o'clock in the afternoon, so they let Harmony sleep in.

"Boy, you sure can do some hair," Callie said. Each of them had a hairdo to match their personality, but not to take away from the bride's big debut. Rick decided he'd also do the girls' make-up because Callie wasn't experienced, and she still hadn't been able to find her niche in the make-up compact. Since their dresses were blue satin, Rick gave them cool eyes.

"It is late winter and burgundy is out of season for good," Rick told Callie.

Asia didn't wear much make-up. She was old-fashioned. Nettie only wore foundation and lip gloss. She didn't mind. She was excited knowing she was wearing it.

After Rick was done with them, he told Asia to wake up the bride. Harmony came in wiping her eyes and smiling. She went to the table to grab a piece of toast. When Harmony saw her girls, she started to cry.

"You three are so beautiful. Dang, Rick! If they look like that, what will I look like?"

"Just sit down and watch me work," Rick said. "Oh, wait. Did you brush your teeth?"

"No. Why?"

"Put down the toast! Go brush your teeth. I don't want nothin' to get in the way. And I especially don't want crumbs in your lipstick when I'm done!"

Harmony did as she was instructed then she went back to Rick's chair. Rick began his creation for Harmony. He did Harmony's hair first. Since her hair had grown back longer than before, he had so many ideas of what he could create.

Harmony's wedding gown was the traditional princess style in the front, but not in the back. She had an opening in the shape of a triangle. The triangle represents the Trinity; The Father, the Son, and the Holy Spirit. It was an Eloise Bay Original, delivered from Sophie's Closet Boutique by the request of the groom. It was the dress she was wearing in John's dream he had while in the hospital after his accident. It was off her shoulders a little and at the reception, she would be able to pull her train up and pin it under so it wouldn't drag on the ground. Her dress was lily white with three bows in the back in three colors; red, white, and yellow. Those were also at the request of the groom.

Rick decided to put Harmony's hair half-up and half-down and he left an area for her to place her veil. He also had what he called "tears of joy" in her hair. It was a style he created just for her. It was breathtaking! He began to cry while he was finishing his masterpiece.

"Now it's time for the make-up," Rick said.

Rick turned Harmony away from the mirror so she couldn't see herself until he was completely done. He gave her waterproof make-up for her eyes because he knew she was going to cry when she saw herself. At Rick's request Asia and Callie had to leave the room while he finished with Harmony. Rick announced that he was finished and asked Harmony if she was ready to see herself.

"Yes!" she replied. Rick turned Harmony to face the mirror. Harmony could not believe what she saw.

"Is that me?" Harmony asked.

"Yes! That is you. And you are beautiful!"

Tears welled up in her eyes and Rick told her not to cry because he didn't want to have to do it all over again. Even though he had used waterproof make-up, he didn't have the strength. He, Harmony and Asia had been friends since they were kids, and this was a special moment for all of them. Rick left to get Asia, Callie, and Nettie.

"Oh my goodness girl! You look magnificent!" Asia said with tears in her eyes.

"I'm jealous and happy at the same time. I can't wait til it's my turn!" Callie said.

"Both of you will have your day. Just be patient." Harmony said.

"It's time to go now." Rick said. "Asia, Callie, let's go! We've got a wedding to attend."

Asia grabbed Harmony's dress and put it in the car. On the drive over, Harmony said thank you to her friends. She handed each of them their gifts and told them not to open them before the wedding. When they arrived at the church Mrs. Sutton met them at the door. Harmony was wearing sweats and a button-down t-shirt.

"Harmony you look nice." Mrs. Sutton said sarcastically.

It was obvious that she had been drinking. Grandma Maddie pushed Mrs. Sutton out of the way and took Harmony's dress into the room where she would finish getting ready.

"Is John here yet?" Harmony asked.

"No, not yet." Mrs. Sutton replied. "Maybe he won't show up," she said under her breath.

"Callie, handle this for me." Grandma Maddie said pointing to Mrs. Sutton.

"I gotcha, Granny. Mrs. Sutton, can I ask you something really quick, please?" Callie said.

"Sure!" Mrs. Sutton replied.

"Follow me."

Callie and Mrs. Sutton left the room. Asia kept watch on them while Harmony was getting dressed. They didn't see Mrs. Sutton again until the ceremony. Grandma Maddie handed Harmony the handkerchief she handmade for her. It was baby blue lace and in the shape of a triangle. Each tip represented a God head in the trinity.

"I know that God sent you to my grandson and I'm glad he waited on the Lord. I'm glad you waited also. Welcome to the family, dear." Grandma Maddie said smiling at Harmony.

Grandpa Rufus came in, and saw them embracing and started crying. He backed out of the door to allow them this private moment. This was a very emotional day for everyone involved.

Mrs. Wilkes came in and asked to be alone with her daughter.

Everyone left the room to give them some privacy.

"Hey baby." Mrs. Wilkes said.

"Hi Ma. Don't cry, please, because I'll cry too. And, Rick will kill me if I mess up my make-up. How's Daddy holding up?"

"He's fine, but he hasn't seen you yet. So who knows what will happen when he does."

"Ma? Is Daddy okay?"

"What do you mean?"

"I mean his health. Is he in good health?"

"Harmony Michelle Wilkes, don't you worry about your father. This is your day; yours and John's."

Just then, there was a knock on the door. It was Mr. Wilkes.

"I'll leave you two alone," Mrs. Wilkes said.

"Hi Daddy." Harmony said. "How do I look?"

"Like a princess," he said. "And, you're getting ready to walk down the aisle to your prince."

"Words can't describe how I feel, Daddy. I'm so happy. And I have joy in my heart right now for John. I'm not even married to him yet and I miss his love."

"I know how you feel because that's how I felt with your mother. No more lectures, just this."

He handed her another gift in a velvet box. It was a tiara. Mr. Wilkes placed it on her head.

"Nothing God ever gave me, except one more day with you, will compare to this moment. I love you, Princess. Or should I say, Mrs. John Sutton, Jr.?"

He gave her a kiss on her cheek; she gave him a kiss on his cheek in return.

"Thank you, Daddy, for everything. I love you for forever and a day."

Mr. Wilkes covered her face with her veil. The veil was at least seven feet long in the back and it hung down to her waist in the front. He walked her to the front of the church. All of the wedding party had already gone in. Nettie looked so pretty at the front of the church. She was smiling at some of the boys down front.

"Well, she may not give her candy away, but she doesn't mind letting them look at her wrappers," Harmony thought to herself. A song began to play that was not familiar to either John or Harmony. Before Harmony entered the room, she looked down the aisle and saw that Jacob and Charles placed a poster-size picture of James on the end. This was the surprise they had for John. As Harmony and her father entered the sanctuary, blue and white rose pedals fell from the ceiling. It looked as if it were snowing in the church. John began to cry. Jacob was crying as well. Charles handed both of them a tissue. As Mr. Wilkes walked her down the aisle he told Harmony this is the song he and her mother danced to on their wedding day.

"It's beautiful Daddy."

Before Mr. Wilkes gave his little girl's hand to John, he whispered something in Harmony's ear. John and Harmony looked at Mr. Wilkes a little perplexed.

"I will always be your princess, Daddy and thank you for giving me away to my second prince."

She gave him a hug and Mr. Wilkes gave Harmony's hand to John. No one heard what Mr. Wilkes said except Harmony. John took Harmony's hand and the ceremony began. The ceremony lasted twenty minutes. When the minister said that John could finally kiss his bride, he started to cry. He kissed her on the forehead first, and then he kissed her on the mouth for what seemed like an eternity.

After the ceremony and many pictures, they headed to the reception. Dinner consisted of baked Cornish hens, stuffed with potatoes. A vegetable medley and Hawaiian rolls along with Grandma Maddie's famous peach cobbler were also served. The wedding cake had three tiers. One tier was trimmed in yellow roses, another had white roses, and the third tier had little red roses. John's grandparents paid for the cake. John and Harmony didn't do all of the traditional things at the reception because John was short on time. He only had a few days home before he had to leave again.

The two traditional things participated in were the father/daughter, mother/son dance, and the money dance. Mr. Wilkes danced with his daughter and while they danced, the song, "Daddy's Little Girl" played. John and his mother danced to a song that had nothing to do with their relationship. Mrs. Sutton was drunk. John was so embarrassed, but that was his mother and he loved her regardless.

After dinner and the money dance, John and Harmony left for their honeymoon. The one, good thing that Mrs. Sutton did for them was to book them into a suite in the most expensive hotel in the downtown area *and* paid for it too. When they arrived, as tradition has it, John picked her up and carried her over the threshold into the room. The rest of the night God blessed them fully; over and over again.

Chapter Fourteen

'TIL DEATH DO US PART...
FORGOTTEN VOWS

A FEW MONTHS PASSED, and the new Mr. and Mrs. Sutton are slowly finding their rhythm as husband and wife. John is out of town. He's been back a couple of times since they were married. There was much work to be done at church and seminary. The hardest part of his schooling was learning Greek.

Mrs. Wilkes called Jacob and Harmony over for a family meeting. Jacob and Harmony arrived at the same time. Jacob has been living with Charles since Harmony got married.

"Do you know what's up?" Harmony asked Jacob.

"No. I thought you'd know."

They walked in and called out to their mother.

"In the kitchen!" Mrs. Wilkes yelled back.

Mr. and Mrs. Wilkes were sitting at the kitchen table. Harmony didn't like the look on their faces.

"Ma, what's wrong?" she asked.

"Sit down you guys. Your father has something he wants to tell you."

Jacob and Harmony sat down next to each other.

"What is it Dad?" Jacob asks.

"I have prostate cancer." Mr. Wilkes said with a shaky voice.

"What? When? How?"

"Hold on Harmony." Mrs. Wilkes said. "Let him answer your questions one at a time."

"I was diagnosed last September."

"Can they treat it Dad?" Jacob asked.

"No Son. It's too advanced."

"I knew it!" Harmony shouted. "I knew something was wrong with you."

With tears in her eyes, Harmony yelled, "Everybody was telling me it was nothing! How could you lie to us like that?! How could you lie to *me* like that Daddy?"

"I didn't want you two to worry. As time passed, and I saw how happy you were I didn't want to ruin your big day, Princess. Please forgive me!" her father cried.

"I promised I wouldn't say anything until after the wedding." Mrs. Wilkes said.

"Well, what do we do now Dad?"

"We wait, Son."

"How long?" Harmony asked.

"At the time, the doctor gave him a year, but it's progressing quickly and he's getting weaker." Mrs. Wilkes said. "I know what you're thinking. He didn't want to do surgery or chemo."

"It's all in God's hands now, baby." Mr. Wilkes stated.

Harmony ran up to her old room and called John. She gave him the news and they cried together on the phone. He couldn't talk long so he prayed with her and told her he'd call her later tonight. Then Harmony called Asia and Rick. They were speechless. All they could do was cry with her.

Uncle Lionel called and asked if the kids had been told yet.

"Uncle Lionel knew? That's why you picked up the phone so quick when he asked about Dad. Aw, Ma. Couldn't we have done anything differently to help him?"

"No, Harmony. Your father didn't want to bother with that. He said he'd let the Lord decide for him. You know how stubborn he is and when he makes up his mind, he's done with it."

Harmony and Jacob went over to their father and let him know that they'd do everything they could to help.

"Don't go babyin' me." Mr. Wilkes said shrugging them off. "I still have my pride. You kids keep living your lives. Your mother will let you know when to come over."

"Pop. What do we do? How do we do for both of you?" Jacob asked.

"You go on home now. God knows." Mrs. Wilkes said assuredly.

"So just like that we have to leave and act as if you didn't just tell us that news?" Harmony shouted!

"Harmony Michelle Wilkes! Princess! Go home!" Mr. Wilkes said in a weak, quivering voice.

"Let's go Sis." Jacob said.

Before Harmony walked out the door she turned to her parents and shook her head at them in disbelief. She forced the door open angrily, got into her car then left. On the way home all she could think of was how much loss she has suffered in her life. First there was Tony, Uncle Lionel's wife, and now her father.

"It isn't fair Lord." She cried out. "Why him? Why me? What am I gonna do without my Daddy?"

When Harmony arrived home she turned on one light in the front room, went to the couch and continued crying until she fell asleep.

Harmony tried to keep herself busy at work in order to take her mind off of the fact that her father was dying, and her husband was out of town for at least another three weeks. She got involved with the children and youth at the church like she and John had talked about. There was so much work to do that she had to call in some help. She asked Callie and Charles to come in and help her facilitate classes. Charles would teach the boys and Callie and Harmony would take the girls. Together, they developed a teaching strategy and scheduled meeting times with Pastor Sutton. Harmony and Pastor Sutton met for a few minutes alone before the next class.

"Harmony, how's your father?" Pastor Sutton asked.

"He's holding on Mr. Sutton."

"How are you holding up?"

"I'm fine, I guess."

He came over and gave her a hug.

"God knows what he's doing. Trust that He does."

"Thanks Pastor." Harmony replied.

Mrs. Sutton came into the room and saw them talking.

"Hi Harmony, I'm sorry to hear about your father. John filled us in on the details."

"Thank you, Mrs. Sutton."

"And I'm sorry about my behavior on your wedding day, too."

"Apology accepted, Mrs. Sutton."

"Call me Meredith, please."

"Uh, no, I think Mrs. Sutton would be better. I have to get back to my class. I'll talk with you all later."

Mrs. Sutton looked at Pastor Sutton with a perplexed look on her face.

"What do you expect Meredith? Pastor Sutton said. "The girl knows you don't like her. You can't have it both ways."

Mrs. Sutton walked out of the room feeling dismissed.

Time felt like it passed slowly and quickly at the same time for Harmony's family. It felt as if all of this was a horrible dream. The third week John returned home, Mr. Wilkes had become gravely ill. Nurses came and went throughout the day and night to make sure Mr. Wilkes was comfortable. Jacob and Harmony never left their father's side. Mr. Wilkes requested to speak to his family in private. The nurses left the room.

His words to Belle were for her to be strong and to take care of herself and that he loved her dearly. He also told her thank you for loving him even when he messed up. When Harmony heard this she twisted her face wondering what he meant. He told Jacob to take care of his sister and his mother, and to let God choose his wife. For Harmony, he mustered up enough breath in his lungs to sing her a song. It was the one that he sang to her mother when she was pregnant with her, and it made her jump in the womb. All of them began to cry.

Mr. Wilkes died surrounded by his family. Harmony wouldn't let the coroner take his body until she was ready to let go. And since that time would never come, they had to physically pick her up and take her out of the room. Harmony didn't say another word for quite some time. John came by the Wilkes' home and all she could do was cry in his arms. She cried so much that John had to change his shirt. While planning the funeral service they stumbled across old photos of them with their dad when they were little. This was all too much for Harmony to deal with so she let her mother and Jacob do the planning.

The funeral was at John's father's church because it could hold a lot more people. The service was upbeat and inspirational. Uncle Lionel sang "Amazing Grace," and Jacob read a poem. Though the eulogy was short Pastor Sutton spoke of Mr. Wilkes as being a man for God's plan. Harmony was quiet through the entire service, but nodded to Pastor Sutton as a thank you. The repast was held at the Wilkes' Home.

Harmony still wasn't speaking to anyone regarding her father's passing, not even to her husband. John had to leave the day after tomorrow. He tried to help make sense of it for Harmony, but he couldn't. Harmony wouldn't eat and John began to worry.

"She'll be okay." Mr. Sutton said to John. "She just needs time."

It was time for John to leave again and Harmony gave him a long hug and kiss good-bye.

"I love you, you know. Call me if you need to talk. I'll call you when I get in." Harmony nodded yes and let John's hand go. Harmony went back to work a few days later. She was informed that she had to take a trip to Chicago. She welcomed the trip because she needed to get out of town. She told Jacob and her mother where she'd be and called John to inform him.

"How are you Michelle?"

"I'm fine. How's school?"

"Good."

"I have to go now John. I have to pack my bags. I'm on the red-eye tonight."

"Okay," John said. "Call me la---."

She hung up the phone before he could finish and began to pack. While Harmony was away in Chicago, she went for dinner at a local soul food restaurant called "Classics." It received four stars on the review list in her hotel room for eateries. She hadn't really eaten anything for a few days and she was starving for some home cooking. The ambiance was electric. There was a jazz quartet in the far corner, and they all stood under a light blue light. Each member wore black and their instruments were brass. There was a tenor saxophonist, drummer, piano player, and a singer. The entire room had a vibe that made you not only want to sit down, but stay.

Each table had numbers on them and a tea light in the center to set the mood. Couples were linked up by their hands, arms, legs, or whatever kept them close. Everyone, including the single people in the room, swayed to the beat as if they were all somehow connected. Harmony recognized the song that was playing. It was the song her father sang to her right before he died. Harmony began to cry. Just then, an African-American gentleman standing 6'6", weighing 240 pounds, all muscle, athletic-type stopped by her table to see what was wrong. She looked up and it was someone she had known since she was twelve years old.

"Harmony?"

"Trevor?"

"Oh my goodness, what are you doing in Chicago?" he asked.

"I'm here on business."

"What about you?"

"I'm here on business, too. How's the family?"

"Okay, except my father died a couple weeks ago."

"Oh, I'm sorry to hear that. Is that why you were crying?"

"Yes." she said.

"I remember your dad used to chase me down the street with a belt because I'd hit you."

They both laughed.

"Yeah, he said it was because you liked me, but I didn't believe it."

"Well, he was right."

Trevor sat down in the chair next to her, wiped her tears from her face and smiled at her.

"What else is going on in your life?"

Trevor turned away to look at the jazz band for a quick moment, and that gave Harmony the opportunity to turn her wedding ring around so that he couldn't see it. For some odd reason she was mad at John.

"Not much really. Just trying to make it in this world. I really miss my dad."

"Hey, whatever happened to Asia, your best friend?" he asked.

"She lives twenty minutes from me." Harmony replied.

"And Rick?"

"He's about the same distance away. We're still the best of friends. They were in my wedding."

"Your *wedding*?" He replied in shock.

Realizing she had opened her mouth too soon, with a little embarrassment, she said, "Yes, I'm married now."

"Congratulations!" he said to her. "He's a very lucky man."

Harmony giggled and directed her eyes to the jazz band.

"What does your husband do?"

"He's a minister."

"Wow! And you're in here? Isn't that a sin or something?"

"Or something," she said with a grimace. "It was good to see you again, Trevor. I need to go back to my room now. I don't feel too good."

"You want some help?"

"No. I can make it, thanks."

Just as she approached the door, she lost her balance. Trevor rushed over to help her. He walked her back to her hotel room and helped her sit on the couch.

"Are you okay?" He asked.

"I haven't eaten anything for a few days. And I opted to have a drink on top of that. Not a good move on my part."

Trevor got her a glass of water and just as she drank it, she ran to the bathroom to throw up. This was an image of Harmony that he had never seen. She was always the good girl in school. Harmony made her way back to the couch and began to ask Trevor a series of questions as a distraction.

"You said you were here on business. What kind of business do you do?"

"I work as a representative for a pharmaceutical company. I basically buy and sell drugs - legally."

"How crazy! You look good for a drug dealer. How are your parents?"

"Divorced, but still sleeping together. I guess that was in the settlement."

They both laughed.

"I'm sorry that you had to see me like that Trevor. The past few months have been difficult."

"It's okay. We all have our bad days. So when do you fly back home? He asked?"

"Tomorrow night. And you?"

"I don't leave until next week. Hey, let me give you my card and if you're in Chicago again call me up to see if I'm here. I fly in here at least three times a month."

"Okay, thanks. It was great seeing you again."

"You haven't changed a bit, Harmony. Still that little girl I remember socking in the arm, and just as pretty."

Harmony began to doze off on Trevor's arm. She looked peaceful. Trevor gave her room on the couch to stretch out; he covered her with a blanket, then left.

The next morning, Harmony's head was pounding and she had a hard time getting ready for her meeting. Upon arriving to the meeting, she asked for a cup of strong, black coffee. The meeting was long and boring, and Harmony did all she could to stay alert. As soon as the meeting was over she went to get something to eat at the deli on the first floor of the hotel. All she could stand to eat and drink were toast and tea. She reached into her purse for a mirror to see how she looked. Just as she thought, she looked hung over; dark circles around her eyes, puffy cheeks, and pale faced. Talking to herself out loud, she said, "Last night was not a good idea, young lady. You know better!"

Harmony had to rush back to her room to pack her bags and check-out of the hotel. Her plane was scheduled to leave in four hours, and the airport was an hour away. On the flight home, all Harmony thought about was seeing John. But then she remembered he wasn't home yet. She decided to go visit her mom before going home.

"Ma? Is anyone here?" Harmony shouted.

"In the kitchen!" Mrs. Wilkes shouted back. "Hi baby. How was your trip?"

"It was okay Ma. What are you doing?"

"Not much of anything." Mrs. Wilkes replied. "I'm just trying to stay busy by reorganizing shelves in the kitchen, cleaning out the garage, and other odd jobs that your father used to do. I really miss him. We always had so much fun together."

"Ma, do you want me to stay with you tonight?"

"I'll be fine," Mrs. Wilkes replied. "Besides, Jacob is home again. He and Charles had a falling out because Charles kept preaching to him about his lifestyle choices."

"What?" Harmony hollered.

"Your brother is lonely and misses your father and I think he's just run amuck looking for love. All I can do at this point is pray for him 'cause he doesn't listen to me. Maybe you can get through to him."

"I'll deal with my brother another time. Are you sure you don't need me to do anything?"

"No baby. Go on home. I'm sure you're tired."

"I am Ma. I need to get some sleep. I'll call you tomorrow. I love you and try and get some rest."

"I love you too. Good night baby." Mrs. Wilkes said.

"Nite, Ma."

Harmony left heading home. When she arrived she went straight to bed. She didn't even say her prayers or listen to the answering machine.

Harmony awoke in the middle of the night because she thought she heard someone in the front room. She sat up in the bed and went to reach for the bat that she had placed under her side of the bed. It was there for her to defend herself when John was away. She thought she heard footsteps coming toward her room so she got up and stood behind the door. Just as her door opened, she swung and hit the person in the stomach.

"Ahhh!" he screamed. "Harmony?"

"John? What are you doing home?"

"Didn't you get my message on the machine?"

"No. I didn't check the messages. Oh baby, I'm sorry. Let me help you to the bed."

"Why do you have that bat?"

"It's for protection."

She gave him a huge kiss on his tummy to make it feel better.

"It hurts on my head, too," he said sounding wounded. She kissed him there also. He pointed to his lips and said, "It hurts here too." So she kissed him and apologized and before they knew it, the sun had come up.

"Good morning, Husband. How did you sleep?"

"Fine, after my stomach got better."

"How were you able to get away from school?"

"I practically begged for them to let me leave. I missed you so much I couldn't concentrate. The director saw how hard this was on me. He offered me a chance to go to school part-time and that way I could be home a little more."

"But how long will it take you to finish?"

"It will add another two years to my program."

"But if you keep going at the rate you're going, you'd be finished when?"

"One more year." John stated.

"Well, I say stick to what you're doing. I'll be fine. I miss you too, but if you go ahead and get it done, you can be home sooner. Our money situation is fine."

Harmony walked over to hug and reassure her husband that she would be okay.

"How have you been lately Michelle? The death of your father took a toll on you. You really had me scared for you; for us."

"I'm sorry for that," she sighed. I just couldn't imagine my father not being here anymore. In my eyes he was still so young. But he was stubborn and didn't take care of himself like he should have. I'm going to make sure you take care of yourself, John, so you won't end up dying early like my father."

"How's your mom?"

"She's okay. She's staying busy, but she misses him a lot."

"And what about Jacob?"

"That boy's doing his own thing. It's a wonder he still has a job. Ma wanted me to talk to him, but I haven't had a chance to get over there yet."

"Let me talk to him, Harm. Maybe he needs a man to talk to."

"Okay." Harmony said. "I'm going to get in the shower."

A couple hours later, John went over to talk to Jacob. It turned out that Jacob was using anything and anyone he could to cover his pain from the loss of his father.

"Jacob, you can't keep going like this man. It's not good for your health and you're going to lose your job. Your mother is worried sick about you and Harmony's about to come over and kick your butt." John said.

Jacob started to cry and told John how much he missed his father. "He was my best friend and I never told him."

"I'm sure he knew." John said.

They hugged one another until Jacob stopped crying.

"Let's get something to eat."

"You didn't eat breakfast, John?"

"Naw, man. Your sister wouldn't let me."

They just laughed and went out to eat.

"Thanks John for talking to me today. I appreciate you embracing the big brother role with me."

"Big brother?" John said.

"Yea, well, you know you're a few years older than I am."

"Whatever. You take care of yourself man, and go see your mom. She's worried about you."

"I will," Jacob said. "See ya."

John had to leave the next evening. On the way to the airport he and Harmony held hands in the car and talked about how they met and their dating season. She stopped the car in front of the porter station. Harmony wouldn't let John leave.

"Remember, it's better this way." John said.

"I know. That doesn't mean I have to like it. Call me when you get in if you can." Harmony said.

"Okay. I love you Michelle."

"I love you too, John."

She watched his plane take off then she left. On the way home Harmony's cell phone rang. It was her secretary.

"Mrs. Sutton, this is Charmaine."

"Hello Charmaine. How are you?"

"I'm great thank you. Just letting you know that you need to be on the four o'clock flight to Chicago tomorrow evening."

"Okay. Can you fax me my itinerary?"

"It's already done."

"Thank you, Charmaine."

Harmony hung up the phone and got excited about going to Chicago again. She looked in her purse and pulled out Trevor's card and gave him a call. He didn't pick up so she left him a message saying she'd be in town tomorrow night, and asked if he wanted to grab something to eat? She hung up the phone and went home to pack.

As always, Harmony flew First Class. She decided to have one glass of champagne with strawberries. She and John had tried it on their honeymoon. Harmony liked it, but John didn't. After getting settled in her hotel room, she saw that she had two missed calls on her cell phone. The first was from John. He left a message saying he loved her and that he got in safely, and he apologized for not calling sooner but he had trouble as soon as he landed and that he would talk to her about it later. The next message was from Trevor. He told her dinner would be fine, but he couldn't get there until ten. That was fine with her because she needed to freshen up.

Harmony and Trevor met at Classics again, but this time she wasn't sick or crying. She dressed modestly and covered all the key areas as not to attract any unnecessary attention. When Trevor arrived he was wearing a long-sleeved, white, buttoned-down Josh Be. Dress shirt. He was also wearing a black Abram Martin jacket. No tie and black slacks. The cologne he wore had a fragrance that drew you in; almost enticing her.

"Remember, you're a happily married girl," she told herself.

They greeted one another with a hug. In concert they asked each other how their day went.

"Ladies first!" Trevor said.

"I'm good. My husband was able to come home this past week, so that was good. Feeling a bit awkward for sharing that information she asked, "How about you?"

"Not much for me, just work."

"All work and no play make Trevor a dull boy."

"Yeah well, I don't have much time to date anyone. I haven't been lucky enough to find someone like you."

"You don't even know me anymore. It's been years since we've seen each other."

"Well, I know that you have a beautiful smile; you're sexy, smart, a fighter and dedicated to your job and family."

Harmony blushed.

"Oh. And, you can't hold your liquor either.

"Ah yes, a rare quality. Will you excuse me Trevor? I have to go to the ladies room."

He watched her walk away, and licked his lips. Harmony's cell phone rang, and Trevor looked to see who it was. The screen said "husband.". Trevor decided to answer her phone.

"Hello?"

"Hello? I must have the wrong number. This is my wife's phone. Is Harmony around?" John asked.

"Um, she went to the ladies room. May I ask whose calling?"

"This is her husband. Who's this?"

"This is her friend."

"Her friend, who?"

Trevor hung up the phone without answering him, and erased the evidence of John's phone call. Harmony returned to the table and they finished their conversation.

"Anything interesting happen while I was away?" she asked.

"Nah, nothing." Trevor replied.

They finished their meal, had dessert and danced to songs they hadn't heard since their high school days. They were having a great time. Harmony was smiling and laughing again and she felt alive. After the dance, they went back to their table. Harmony realized that it was getting late and she had an early meeting in the morning. Trevor paid for their meals and Harmony paid the tip. As they were leaving the restaurant, she looked up and saw Shondra coming in with a man Harmony had never seen before.

"This does not look good," Harmony thought.

She was embarrassed. She had been spotted with another man while she was out of town and her husband was away. What in the world is she going to do to keep Shondra quiet? Harmony knew Shondra did not like her; especially after what happened with Jacob and him going to jail. He had to pay $3,000 in court fees and restitution for the fight at the club.

"Well, well, well Mrs. Sutton, what brings you here?" Shondra asked.

"I had a meeting with a client." Harmony responded.

"A client? Is *that* what it's called these days? No, Harmony," Shondra said, "*This* is a client," pointing to her date.

Shondra started to walk away. As she's walking away, she whispered in Harmony's ear, "I can't wait to hear what your husband says when he finds out about your *client.*" For the first time since her father died, Harmony stood in fear.

"Who is that?" Trevor asked.

"Satan's helper." Harmony answered.

"I don't understand." He said.

"Trevor, I have to go. I have to go now!"

Trevor put Harmony in a cab and she went back to her hotel room, alone.

During her meeting the next day, all Harmony could think about was the exchange between her and Shondra. She had to tell John before Shondra did. John wouldn't be back for a week or so, and Harmony didn't want to tell him something like this over the phone. She decided to wait until he got home and tell him face to face.

After Harmony arrived home from her business trip, she called her mother to let her know that she had arrived home safely, and she was going to bed because she was tired. Plus, she had to get ready for church service in the morning. Harmony didn't sleep well that night. So many scenarios ran through her mind about how to deal with Shondra. The next thing Harmony heard was her alarm clock going off at 6 am. She got out of bed and got ready for church.

At church, Pastor Sutton preached from Genesis 3:1-7. His title was "Playtime is Over." He talked about how the serpent is there to teach us a lesson. The three points Pastor Sutton used were: We are distracted by the wrong attractions and what is forbidden. The second one was: Interacting with the wrong faction. How we are not focused and how sin is addictive and so is sinful behavior. And the third point was: Contractions because of our wrong reaction. We've been bitten and we justify what we're doing. Then we ask ourselves, "How did we get here?" That's exactly what Harmony was thinking about what happened with Trevor. Nothing actually happened she thought, but if she allows Shondra to tell the story, she will make it seem like she and Trevor were deep in sin.

In closing, Pastor Sutton said, "Wrong begins the minute you stop doing right." Harmony went over to her father-in-law and asked him if he'd heard from John. Pastor Sutton said he hadn't. She asked Mrs. Sutton and she said John called her last night and shared some information with her that caught her by surprise.

"Really?" Harmony asked.

"Yes. Is there anything you care to share with me dear?"

"Um, no Mrs. Sutton. I have to go," Harmony said. "I'll talk to you later."

Harmony called Asia and told her to meet her at her mother's house.

"Ma's cooking pot roast."

"Oh Lord, this is serious. I'm on my way."

When Asia arrived at the Wilkes home, Mrs. Wilkes told Asia to sit down and tell her what's been going on in her life lately. Asia told Mrs. Wilkes that everything was going well, and that she really needed to talk to Harmony right now about girl stuff. Mrs. Wilkes excused her to go upstairs to talk to Harmony. Harmony told Asia everything that happened with Trevor in Chicago and Shondra seeing her walk out of the club with him.

"Girl, I thought Trevor and his family moved to another country." Asia said.

"No, he moved to New York and finished school there and became a sales representative for a pharmaceutical company. He was in Chicago on business when I saw him the first time, accidentally.

The second time we met up for dinner on purpose. We danced and had a good time. And that's all. We were leaving and that's when we saw Shondra and *her* date. Asia, I need to get to John. I think Shondra has already told him and his family what she saw and probably put her own spin on things."

Harmony began to pace the floor.

"What am I going to do?" Harmony asked.

"Let's pray, girl."

"You want to pray?" Harmony asked.

"I do pray! Not as much as I should, but I do. Come on!" Asia grabbed Harmony's hands and began to pray.

"Lord Jesus, my friend and I need your help right now. Please don't let Shondra tell John what she saw. Amen!"

"That was too pitiful, Asia. Let's do it again." Harmony began to pray.

"Father, I stretch my hand to thee; no other help I know. Lord, I have done wrong in your eyes and I ask that you forgive me for that. I want to make you proud in everything that I do, say and think. Please, hold Shondra's tongue for me in order that I might tell my husband the truth. And Lord, please give him the spirit of calm to receive this information as I have intended. Amen."

"Why did you call him in the first place?" Asia asked.

"I don't know. I was bored, and girl, he looked and smelled so good. You know John doesn't like to dance, but that's beside the point."

Harmony's cell phone rang.

"It's Trevor. What do I do?"

"Don't answer it."

Harmony answered and put him on speaker phone so Asia could hear the conversation.

"Hello?

"Hi gorgeous! Trevor said.

"Trevor, how are you?"

"I'm good, real good. When are you going to be in Chicago again?"

"Um, no time soon, why?"

"I'd like to have dinner with you again and reminisce."

Just then Harmony turned off the speaker phone, but kept the receiver tilted so Asia could hear.

"Trevor, I, um, well…"

Asia socks Harmony on the arm to remind her of what they just talked about.

"I don't think that would be a good idea, Trevor. I'm married and I need to keep myself out of places that are questionable, and with other men."

"Okay. I get it. It was good to see you."

"Thank you for understanding."

"Okay, you take care." Trevor said.

"You too Trevor."

Harmony hung up the phone.

"What else did he say?" Asia asked.

"You heard him. He wanted to have dinner again the next time I fly to Chicago."

"Harmony, you have to leave him alone!"

"Asia, I haven't done anything wrong. Now, you have to help me keep Shondra quiet."

"But we just prayed about it. Leave it to God. Hey, wait a minute! Why do you need to keep her quiet if you're not up to anything?"

Harmony turns away from her friend.

"John will understand when you tell him. Won't he?" Asia asked.

"That's not good enough!" Harmony yelled. "Are you going to help me or not?"

"Yeah, girl. I got your back no matter what. Don't screw up what you have with John."

"Don't worry, I won't, but I'm going to fix Shondra's wagon and paint it red when I see her."

While Harmony and Asia were trying to come up with a plan Harmony's cell phone rang. It was John.

"Should I answer it? Harmony asked.

"Yes, you should answer the call from your husband."

Harmony answered the phone on speaker.

"Hello?"

"Hi Harmony. You busy?"

"Hi John. How are you? No. I'm never too busy for you."

"Hmm. Alright." John says. "I'm coming home on a flight tonight. Can you pick me up from the airport?"

"Of course. Is everything ok?" She asked.

"I hope so Harmony. We'll talk when I get there. See you tonight."

Before Harmony could say anything else John hung up the phone.

"Oh my goodness Asia! Do you think Shondra already told him?"

"I don't know. Do you want to pray again?" Asia asked feeling lucky.

"No. No time. I gotta get outta here, get home and be ready to greet my man in some lingerie. Surely he won't fuss at me if he sees me in something sexy right?"

"I don't know. I don't have a man." Asia stated.

Breathing heavily Harmony says, "I need to think. I'll call you later."

"Okay. Call me later girl."

Harmony leaves so quick she forgets to tell her mom she was leaving.

"Where's your friend?" Mrs. Wilkes asked.

"She went home Mrs. Wilkes. She has a clean-up on aisle seven."

"A what?" Mrs. Wilkes asked.

"Nothing. I'm being silly. Good seeing you again Mrs. Wilkes. Bye."

"Bye Asia. Drive safe."

Mrs. Wilkes began cleaning the living room when her phone rang. It was Mrs. Sutton.

"Hello?"

"Belle Wilkes please?"

"This is Belle Wilkes. Who's calling please?"

"Hi. Mrs. Wilkes? This is Meredith Sutton, John's mother. We need to talk."

Printed in the United States
By Bookmasters